BACKSTAGE P.

Memoirs of an American Snowman

By

Frank Lynch

TIRED BUZZARD PUBLISHING COMPANY

KILLARNEY, FLORIDA

IN COOPERATION WITH

TRAFFORD PUBLISHING COMPANY

VICTORIA, BC, CANADA

Order this book online at www.trafford.com
or email orders@trafford.com

Most Trafford titles are also available at major online book retailers.

Note for Librarians: A cataloguing record for this book is available from Library and Archives Canada at www.collectionscanada.ca/amicus/index-e.html

Printed in Victoria, BC, Canada.

ISBN: 978-1-4120-2743-4 (Soft)

We at Trafford believe that it is the responsibility of us all, as both individuals and corporations, to make choices that are environmentally and socially sound. You, in turn, are supporting this responsible conduct each time you purchase a Trafford book, or make use of our publishing services. To find out how you are helping, please visit www.trafford.com/responsiblepublishing.html

Our mission is to efficiently provide the world's finest, most comprehensive book publishing service, enabling every author to experience success. To find out how to publish your book, your way, and have it available worldwide, visit us online at www.trafford.com

Trafford rev. 8/27/2009

 www.trafford.com

North America & international
toll-free: 1 888 232 4444 (USA & Canada)
phone: 250 383 6864 ♦ fax: 812 355 4082 ♦ email: info@trafford.com

This book is dedicated to my long suffering wife, Barbara, and my fantastic daughters, Shannon and Diana; thanks you three for allowing me to live my dreams and to P.T. Barnum for inspiring those dreams.

AUTHOR'S NOTES

These are the actual experiences and history of Frank Lynch and this book reflects his opinion of the past, present and future. The personalities, events, actions and conversations portrayed within the story have been reconstructed from his memory, extensive interviews, and research, utilizing press accounts, court documents, letters, personal papers, and the memories of participants. In an effort to safeguard the privacy of certain individuals, the author has changed their names and, in some cases, altered other identifying characteristics. Events involving the characters happened as described; only minor details have been altered.

This book, much like a circus, contains two parallel story lines. If read from front to back cover you are reading my autobiography much like a circus has a general theme. It can also be enjoyed by reading the chapters on the entertainers you are most interested in first and hopscotching from story to story, as each stands on its own as an amusing true story in the annals of entertainment history, just as each performer's act in a circus stands on its own. Either way, I hope you will find it a most enjoyable read.

TABLE OF CONTENTS

Introduction

Ninety-nine percent of you reading this book have picked it up because you are interested in the entertainment personalities you have seen mentioned either on the cover or in the following pages of this manuscript. Since I was fortunate enough to have worked with them all, a bit about me and how this book came to be seem apropos.

Three factors spurred me to write this behind the scenes look into the entertainment world. The original idea came from the many people who have interviewed me over the years for their own books about performers I have worked with. Authors on books about Elvis Presley, Michael Jackson, and the rock band Lynyrd Skynyrd, as well as many newspaper, radio, and television reporters have sought me out for backstage stories and many suggested I write my own story.

Secondly, so many people over the years have asked "What was it like meeting (insert name of your favorite celebrity)? What was (insert name again) really like?" Now all the stories are collected in one place for all to read and that question can hopefully be answered, at least in the time I was lucky enough to be with them.

Lastly, because of the era I happened to live in I was fortunate enough to do things in one lifetime that others could only dream about. I'm not sure there is another person alive who can say they worked with both Elvis Presley AND Michael Jackson as well as all the others. This book serves as a testament to the times and a life story that no one else could equal. I have been very fortunate, not only to have lived the following pages but to have been able to publish that story for my family, friends and generations to come.

The stories you are about to read are all true and come from my four decades in the entertainment industry. My positions ranged from backstage manager at various arenas to the owner/operator of The All-American Flea Circus.

A resume makes for poor and boorish reading but a short list here can be used for reference later or perhaps you will think back to a time and place mentioned and realize we may have crossed paths before!

THE BATH & TENNIS CLUB & HOTEL
WESTHAMPTON BEACH, NY

Working with: Don Rickles, Cary Grant, Bricktop, Hugh Shannon, Lionel Hampton, Steve Lawrence and Edie Gorme, Uriah Heep, Jackie Onassis, et al.

THE HOLLYWOOD SPORTATORIUM
HOLLYWOOD, FLORIDA

Working with: Elvis Presley, Bob Dylan, Bruce Springsteen, Patti Smith, Boston, ELO, Lynyrd Skynyrd, Parliament-Funkadelic, America, ZZ Top, KISS, George Foreman, NWA Wrestling with Dusty Rhodes, Killer Karl Kox, Gordon Solie and Eddie & Mike Graham, Pistol Pete Maravich & the New Orleans Jazz, Pink Floyd, Neil Young, Dr. Hook, Shirley "Cha Cha" Muldowney and the NHRA and scores of others.

ORANGE COUNTY CONVENTION CENTER
ORLANDO, FLORIDA

Working with: Billy Joel, Bob Barker, Willie Nelson, Jackson Browne, the Harlem Globetrotters, Ringling Bros. and Barnum & Bailey Circus, Kenny Rogers, Victor the Rasslin' Bear and more!

SIX FLAGS/20TH CENTURY FOX
ORLANDO, FLORIDA

Working with: Michael Jackson, Danny Thomas, John Anderson, Terri Gibbs, Lee Greenwood, Bill Monroe, all in real life AND hundreds of more stars in wax in the world's largest wax museum at Six Flags Stars Hall of Fame.

CENTROPLEX SPECIAL EVENTS
ORLANDO, FLORIDA

Working with: The Rolling Stones, Van Halen, Hank Williams Jr., The Who, John Cougar Mellancamp, B52's, Joan Jett, The O'Jays, Luther Vandross, Bill Cosby, Tone-Loc, Downtown Julie Brown, Milli Vanilli, Hulk Hogan, Andre The Giant and others.

Add to that, stints as manager of the Elvis Presley Museum and Ripley's Believe It Or Not! Museum and as owner of the Rock 'N' Roll Museum, Shandi Amusements, Lynch Family Entertainment, and Lynch Combined Shows and you can see it has not been an ordinary run-of-the-mill life.

I have attended Super Bowls, including being on the field for Super Bowl XIII, sat front row for an NBA final game with rapper Flavor Flav, white water rafted the Grand Canyon, skated in the Roller Derby, and taken a pie in the face in the center ring of the Ringling Bros. Circus. I appeared in the movie *Matinee* with John Goodman and Jesse White, wrestled a bear, dined in a fine restaurant with a chimpanzee, been in a cage with tigers, and trained and presented monkey acts.

All of this has a common thread, believe it or not. I have been and am fascinated by people who can move a crowd to emotion or applause and have worked with some of the best at this including faith healers, superstar entertainers, circus performers and professional wrestlers. Having hosted the 20th Century Fox Screen Test Theater in Orlando, Fla., doing eight live shows a day, I know how addicting the energy and applause of a crowd can be. Having walked some of the greatest entertainers of all time to their stage, that emotion, energy and applause put forth by a crowd is something, that once experienced, can never be forgotten.

To this day, my mother laments not having forced me to go to the opera and ballet as a child. I was always much more interested in when the circuses were coming to town, or watching the wrestlers on television. I admire P.T. Barnum as others do statesmen or other more traditional heroes. So along that line, "Step right up, the big show is on the inside!" Join me in this big show called my life, find out about some of the best and worst performers of all time, have a few laughs along the way and remember to always take the path of most enjoyment because life is always too short.

CHAPTER 1
I KNOW IT'S ONLY ROCK 'N ROLL

I am always asked how I became a backstage manager. My entry into this aspect of the entertainment world was simply being in the right place at the right time (and unwittingly being the right size). Prior to attending Biscayne College in Miami, Florida, in 1975 I had only attended five concerts in my life. Three of those concerts were Elvis Presley concerts, including one of the famous Madison Square Garden concerts of 1972. Little could I have guessed I would be working for him a scant five years later.

After starting college, I applied for a job as a car parker at a new arena opening in Hollywood, Florida, called the Hollywood Sportatorium. The pay was $5 an hour, which was quite a bit of money back then, plus we were told once the cars were parked we could see the shows for free. I was hired as a car parker and arrived for work the first day where the event was the opening day of the Virginia Slims Florida Championships, a professional women's tennis event.

As I walked in, the event's producer was in a heated argument with the building's owner, Norman Johnson about what was being done to provide security for the lady tennis pros, ladies like Billie Jean King and Chris Evert. Mr. Johnson said he would take care of it and looked over his rag tag bunch of car parkers, pointed to the five biggest guys, me being one of them and said "Come to my office."

Once inside, Mr. Johnson said to me, "You! Wherever Chrissie Evert goes for the next five days, you go with her and make sure no one bothers her, understood?"

UNDERSTOOD? As a twenty-year-old guy, I am being given the chance to hang out with an eighteen-year-old multi-millionaire female tennis player AND getting paid for it? What could be better?!

For the next week anytime Chrissie was on property I was with her. She was very nice to me, though I thought a bit short with the fans. I remember her signing autographs when a fan asked, "Did you play your best tennis today?" and she answered very sharply, "I played well enough to win didn't I?" and stormed off. Wrong question, I guess.

There, of course, were lots of other players I got to know a bit including Billie Jean King, Martina Navratilova in her rookie year, Rosie Casals, now in the Tennis Hall of Fame, a great and showy player then, who I played quite a few backgammon games against in the off times and Carol "Spoons" Spooner, the tour trainer and all-around great lady.

At the end of the tournament, which Chris won (she celebrated by unceremoniously tearing the $100,000 presentation check into pieces and tossing it over her head), Norman Johnson, the building's owner came backstage to have his picture taken with her. After the photo he asked her if everything had gone well and she said yes and thanked him. As he turned to leave, he turned to me and said, "You are the new backstage manager. There's a ZZ Top concert here Friday, be here at 5."

And that's how you get to be a backstage manager!

CHAPTER 2
THE ROCK AND ROLL HALL OF FAME

In 2007, I took a look at the inductees in the Rock and Roll Hall of Fame in Cleveland, Ohio, and realized how many of them I was lucky enough to have worked with. Since some may not be mentioned elsewhere in this book, I think it only fitting to list them here for future reference, maybe a future book and most importantly as a tribute to these great stars who I had the privilege of interacting with and seeing perform!

1986	1987
Chuck Berry	The Coasters
James Brown	Bo Diddley
Elvis Presley	Ricky Nelson

1988	1989
The Beach Boys	Dion
The Drifters	The Rolling Stones
Bob Dylan	The Temptations

1990	1993
The Four Seasons	Creedence Clearwater
The Four Tops	Revival
The Temptations	
The Platters	
The Who	

1994	1995
The Grateful Dead	The Allman Brothers
Elton John	Neil Young
Rod Stewart	

1996	1997
David Bowie	Crosby, Stills & Nash
Jefferson Airplane	The Jackson 5
Pink Floyd	Parliament Funkadelic

1998	1999
The Eagles	Billy Joel
Fleetwood Mac	Paul McCartney
Santana	Del Shannon
	Bruce Springsteen

2000

Eric Clapton
Lovin Spoonful
Earth, Wind & Fire
The Moonglows
James Taylor

2001

Aerosmith
Michael Jackson
Queen
Paul Simon
James Burton

2002

Tom Petty
Ramones
Talking Heads

2003

AC/DC
Elvis Costello
The Police

2004

Jackson Browne
Bob Seger
ZZ Top

2005

The O'Jays
The Pretenders
U2

2006

Black Sabbath
Blondie
Lynyrd Skynyrd

2007

Grandmaster Flash &
   the Furious Five
Patti Smith
Van Halen

CHAPTER 3
THE GREAT CHRISSIE EVERT SCAM

Word quickly spread around the small Biscayne College campus where I attended school that I was the appointed bodyguard for Chris Evert at the Hollywood Sportatorium. One person in particular who approached me about it was a guy by the name of Nick Z. Nick was a unique individual with the gift of gab. If you asked him "What's 2 plus 2?" he probably didn't know the answer, but would say "I love addition, it's a great principle of mathematics and a favorite subject of mine, next to my other classes in which I excel as well and I think school is a great learning tool, don't you?" He never gave you the answer and you were never quite sure what he HAD said, but most people just shrugged their shoulders and left it at that.

Nick came to me one day and said "I understand you are working with Chrissie Evert." I said that I was and then he said, "She is my all time favorite. Do you think you could get me an autograph?"

"Sure, Nick," was my response as I knew all I had to do was ask and she would have as she had given me some autographed items earlier in the week.

But then came the kicker. Nick said "I want her to sign it "To the Big Z, with all my love, Chrissie Evert."

Well of course no one in their right mind in my position of working for her would ask her to sign something like that, but my Barnum-esque mind was already hatching a plan and I told him I would get it for him no problem.

The next day I went to Chrissie's dressing room and asked if I could have one of her 8x10 publicity photos. She said I could have as many as I liked so I tucked a few away and went on with the business at hand.

That night when I returned to my dorm room, I took a Sharpie marker and inscribed on the photo "To the Big Z, with all my love, Chrissie Evert." The next day I gave the picture to Nick and he was elated and thanked me profusely. Just the thought of him showing the picture around campus and the fabricated stories I knew he would tell about his "relationship" with Chrissie made me laugh, but the story gets better.

Fast forward five years, and I happen to be attending a party held at Nick Z's house. At one point in the evening he decided to give some of us a tour of his house. In one room hanging on the wall, was the, long forgotten to me, Chrissie Evert picture. "Wow! You know Chris Evert?" I had to ask leadingly.

"Oh sure, I met her while we were in college. We are good friends to this day. She's a great girl and we had a lot of fun together." I managed to keep a straight face, realizing not only that he hadn't remembered who had gotten the picture for him, but also in seeing my handwriting up there displayed so prominently on his wall.

So Nick if you are out there, I hate to burst your bubble after all these years, but that Chrissie Evert autograph is really a Frank Lynch autograph, but maybe it will be worth a little something anyway with the publication of this book.

His pride about that picture reminds me much of a circus sideshow. Even if something isn't really what it was purported to be, if you get some enjoyment out of it anyway, there is really no harm done.

Chris Evert & Author
January 16, 1977

ONE PAGE WONDER

An old carny adage that always applies:

> Of course the game is fixed, but
> you can't win if you don't play.

CHAPTER 4
RICK SPRINGFIELD'S DINNER

I was lucky enough to work with Rick Springfield on his two biggest tours back in the early 1980s. He, of course, had already risen to fame as Dr. Noah Drake on the TV soap opera General Hospital and was much more popular than I would have believed as I had never seen the television show nor had I ever seen him at all until finding myself working for him.

Living in Fort Lauderdale at the time I got a call from John Mazzola the manager of the Florida Citrus Bowl in Orlando asking me if I would be interested in catering the Rick Springfield concert at the Bob Carr Auditorium in Orlando. I had never catered a show before, but readily accepted figuring providing food for a teen idol would be much easier than working as his Backstage manager or security where you are trying to protect him from thousands of teenage (and older) women.

I got the catering supply list which didn't have too many odd demands as was and is in fashion with rock stars (yes, Van Halen wanted M&M candies, but NO brown ones) and found the nearest supermarket and fulfilled the shopping list. I still remember getting into a conversation with the checkout girl and she almost fainting when she found out she was selling me "Rick Springfield's bananas!"

Back at the theater I set up all the food and drink and as it turned out, a band called the U.S. Males, whom I knew, were opening the show, and they were delighted to find out their old friend was the caterer as they could then eat and drink all they cared to. One of the items on the catering list was to deliver Rick Springfield's dinner to his dressing room at 6:30 pm. I had it all prepared and, actually being a good cook, it actually did look very appetizing.

At this time Rick Springfield's album "Working Class Dog" and the huge hit "Jesse's Girl" were out and he was riding a huge surge of popularity. Wanting to make a great impression I hurried down the hall with his dinner in my hot little hands. When I got to his dressing room, there were a few people inside and a person with his back to me blocking the doorway. I said "Excuse me" but the person who was in conversation with the others inside, just ignored me. I once again said "Excuse me!" in a bit louder and more irritated voice, but was once again ignored. Since the contract called for the food to be delivered exactly at 6:30 (and if the show was to go on, I had to get back to the beer cooler and pry the U.S. Males away from it), I pushed the food tray up against the back of the obstinate door blocker and announced loudly and, in retrospect, much too loudly, "Please get out of the way! I have Rick Springfield's dinner here and without it this show won't go on."

The person spun around and said, "Is that so? Do you know who I am?"

I said, "No, but I have to get this dinner to Rick Springfield right now!"

Taking the tray out of my hands with a big smile on his face the reply came, "Well, thanks. I am Rick Springfield, nice to meet you, and you are?"

"Frank," I answered sheepishly. All I can think is that he found it comical and maybe even a bit refreshing that there was someone out there who didn't recognize him and treated him like they would anyone else. He remembered my name and spoke to me the rest of the evening, gave me a laminated all-access backstage pass to be backstage at any of his shows and thanked me for the great food at the end of the night.

Rick's drummer was also a great guy named Jack White, as I remember, and I knew he was cool even before I met him because he wore a white terry cloth robe over his stage outfit. Emblazoned on the back in huge red letters it read:

"THE JACK WHITE SHOW"

and in tiny letters underneath:

"featuring Rick Springfield"

I guess that type of humor kept the band friendly and down to earth because I also remember a song they sang called "It's Springfield, Not Springsteen" because Bruce was incredibly popular at the time and everyone almost unwittingly would say "Rick Springsteen...I mean Springfield." For a rock and roll performer to laugh at that and not take himself too seriously was, and is, refreshing in the biz.

On Rick's next tour I was the backstage manager so, unfortunately, I was much busier than I had been as the caterer the tour prior. I did get to renew old acquaintances and reminded Rick of not recognizing him the last time around but assured him I knew what he looked liked now and we both had a good laugh. I told him I had even purchased his album and he was very sincere in his thanks.

This show was in the much larger Orange County Convention Center in Orlando and as was the practice the crew got free passes (or "comps") to give away as they saw fit. Most of the crew would take theirs out to the lines of ticket buyers and try to entice the pretty (and not so pretty) women with free tickets and promises of backstage access. These types of tickets became known as "orgy comps" in the industry. Although this practice was routine with lots of bands, this was the only show I ever saw where the phrase "orgy comp" was actually printed on the tickets! I still have one of those ticket framed to this day.

It was also at this show I stumbled across one of the female assistants backstage busily signing "Love, Rick Springfield" on his publicity photos. Then, as VIPs and others with backstage passes came back and asked for autographs, this is what they received. Having seen Rick sign a few in his own hand, I must say she was an excellent forger, but I can guarantee there are many more faked signed Rick Springfield autographs out there than there are Chrissie Evert ones!

CHAPTER 5
INTRODUCING...

I always wondered why some performers have great introductions, others horrible ones and others none at all. Great intros always added to the experience, got the crowd incredibly wound up and ready to go without any effort from the performer himself. As you look at professional wrestling today (if you dare), a large part of each wrestler's persona is his intro and intro music taking a lesson from some of the greatest introductions of all time like...

Elvis Presley. The music "Theme From 2001: A Space Odyssey" is certainly one of the most recognizable intro songs in the world. The music itself builds to a great crescendo as does the audience knowing it is announcing the arrival of The King. If you ever experienced Elvis live once in your life, every time you hear that song, you will remember the feeling you had the first time you saw

Elvis walk onto a stage and the incredible energy he brought into an audience. The great professional wrestler Ric "The Nature Boy" Flair used the same music, but even he couldn't match the energy it produced for The King. Elvis, of course, was also perhaps one of the only performers with an ending as well, words that today have become part of the English language meaning goodbye, the simple understatement "Elvis has left the building." And the fact was, (see the Elvis chapter in this book,) he had!

James Brown. This was an introduction that could take up to ten minutes or more! In rap and rhyme it was a running biography of this legendary Hall of Fame performer, listing every song, movie, award, and achievement he had ever received and always included the great line "the hardest working man in America today!" By the time James Brown hit the stage, you'd think the show was half over, but his performance was always a showstopper. Add to that his incredible exhaustion routine, where he fell to the floor, was covered in a gaudy cape and then was helped to his feet, only to grab the mike and start again, he was not just a legendary performer and singer but a great showman as well.

The Shirelles. There was a fantastic movie documentary put out in the mid-1970s called *Let the Good Times Roll.* It was about the then very popular 1950s and 60s rock and roll revival shows going on and the good and bad that went along with them. The soundtrack from the movie is incredible and you can look for the movie every once in a while on the A&E Channel. It lets you see and hear, both onstage and off, legends like Bo Diddley, Chuck Berry, Little Richard, The Five Satins and many others, including the great Shirelles of the song "Soldier Boy" fame. In a sing-songy preacher's voice they were introduced:

Let's get yourself together now,

because it's hit time.

They're known as the hit makers,

record breakers,

money makers.

They have style and grace

and a lovely face.

For all you cats

they're bound to put more dips in your hips,

more cut in your strut,

and more glide in your stride.

They'll make your back crack,

your liver quiver

and your knees freeze.

If you don't dig that

you got a hole in your soul.

If you don't dig this mess,

you came to the wrong address.

Just returned from the stratosphere

they're gonna sing mighty loud and clear.

And when they start to shake

they're gonna cause an earthquake.

While all other groups are laughing and
  joking

Shirelles on the stage, cooking and smoking.

So when I get through rappin'

I want you to start clapping

And put your hands together for

My gals, your gals, everybody's gals...

Let's meet and greet the fabulous
  Shirelles!!!!!!!!!!!!

Try that yourself and see if you can get the rap going, it really is great and a decade before the start of rap music here is something very close, even using the word "rap!" Have I discovered that the Shirelles invented rap music? Okay that might be a stretch, but it still is one of the greatest entertainer intros of all time... now let's hear you!

ONE PAGE WONDER

While taking a college course taught by the legendary Dr. Demie Mainieri, I had missed 2 of the first 3 classes of the year. When I returned to class Doc greeted me with the classic line, "Mr. Lynch, are you taking this class by correspondence?"

CHAPTER 6
FAITH HEALERS, SCENE STEALERS

Among those "entertainers" who can really sway a crowd, I was and am fascinated by the faith healers and other religious fanatics who tend to bring us their message through those 24 hour satellite TV stations. Being from a family of Catholic priests, nuns and fervent believers in Catholicism, family members were always worried when they would walk in on me and see me watching (and enjoying) Jim and Tammy Faye selling their timeshare religion, the Right Reverend Benny Hinn slaying people in the spirit and the Reverend Ernest C. Angely miraculously healing people of every ailment from warts to terminal cancer. Why do these theatrics amuse me? I see them as the new American sideshow. I find little difference between these people and the snake oil salesmen of the Old

West or the sword swallower of the aforementioned circus sideshow. I will not argue whether there is any religious merit to their appearances, but I can tell you from working with them, they put on one hell of a show and, in their ability to move an audience, if nothing else, are great performers.

The Reverend Ernest C. Angely

Perhaps my favorite of all the faith healers is the Reverend Ernest C. Angely. There are so many things about him that make him, in my mind, the best at what he does. First his name, now that took some thought. Is he a Reverend of any kind? Certainly in his own mind, in his own church at least. And is he earnest? From my time with him I found him more fakir than earnest. With no proof I can only suppose he claims the C. to stand for Christ or maybe Cadillac. And that would leave ANGELy to remind us of those angelic spirits who help him heal, in his word, "doctor-sworn incurable cancer." Add to that his unique voice, something of a cross between the voice of the Wicked Witch of the West and fingernails scratching across a blackboard. The kind of voice that would keep you out of any spoken media EXCEPT faith healer TV shows where it works "wonnnnderrrousss miracles." And his crowning touch (literally) is a horrible jet black toupee, more of a full wig really, which is great to watch as he works himself into a full sweat and his wig stays perfectly set in place while the sweat pours out from underneath it.

The only thing I can think of that makes him this bizarre is that he is from Akron, Ohio. Everyone I have ever met or known from Akron seems to "walk to the beat of a different drum." I think it may have to do with the fact Akron for many years produced tires and the smell and pollution of the rubber being processed somehow affected all who lived there. The great country singer/songwriter David Allan Coe (he of the multiple wives and murder charges), the rock group Devo (they of the red flower pots on their heads) and my friend James (JR) Rousmanoff are all from Akron. I rest my case. It was with JR that I set out to meet the Rev.

On the evening Angely was scheduled to appear in Orlando I received a call from JR saying we couldn't miss the show. At the time we were both working for the city and had the keys to the theater he was appearing in and also had use of an undercover police vehicle. The theater is located on the fringe of one of Orlando's poorest areas so before show time we took great delight in rounding corners where the boyz in da hood were out selling their drugs, and flipping on the siren and lights and watching them scatter. We cleared out the front of their local 7-11 in the same manner and then went in and bought some beer.

Arriving back at the theater we entered through a side door, carrying our beer and were greeted by a strange sight. Rev. Angely must not have had a big Orlando following because he had only rented the ground floor of the theater and not the balcony. While the ground floor and stage were awash in theatrical lights, the balcony was closed and pitch black. So again with beer in tow we climbed through the darkness to the front center row of the balcony, best seats in the house and proceeded to watch the show.

The show's beginning was nondescript except for the fact we always had to wait for applause in order to pop the top on our next beer so we wouldn't be found out. The one part I loved was when the Rev started asking for money. "I want everyone who is giving me a thousand dollars tonight to put your hands in the air and wave them back and forth and don't stop! We want a miracle tonight!" A few hands started waving, in my mind, plants (shills) in the audience placed there to encourage others. He continued.. "Now everyone giving $500 or more put your hands in the air, wave them back and forth and don't stop! We want a miracle here tonight!" He continued these instructions for $250 donors, $100, $50, $25, $10 and by his $5 pitch most hands in the congregation were waving. It was at this point Angely said "Anyone who doesn't have their hands up by now, put them up and wave them because you are either so poor or so cheap you truly need a miracle." Great stuff.

Some beers later, came the end of the show when the Rev invited the afflicted to the stage and laid his hands on them in hopes of a miracle cure. He called each affliction by group. "Will everyone with cancer please come to the stage?" Then came blood ailments, leg problems and mental disorders. He then worked each line laying his hands upon people and when he touched them they fell out in a row either in a seemingly dead faint or hitting the floor and flopping around like a hooked fish. What a show!

I had just left the restroom when I heard him call for everyone with back pain to join him onstage. After about 12 beers I considered that my cue. Off to the stage I went. Even the Rev had to notice me, this big hulking white guy in white pants, sandals and Hawaiian print shirt standing in line with this church dressed church going crowd. I remember hoping I could stand still and straight in the line. When the Rev got to me he actually started asking me questions into the mic for the crowd to hear. He either was really stupid or saw the look of another actor in my eye and knew I'd play this to the hilt.

"What's your problem, young man?"

"I hurt my back on the job about three years ago. I can't lift anything, can't touch my toes and my doctor says it's only going to get worse." This was, of course, untrue and off-the-cuff, but since I was in the spotlight…

"And how old are you?" (What's that got to do with anything?)

"Thirty-one."

"Do you believe a miracle can happen tonight?" (Miracle enough might be no hangover the next morning.)

"Yes, sir, I truly do!"

"Ladies and gentlemen, do you think God has the power to heal this young man tonight?" The crowd cheered. "I need some noise to help heal this man!" The crowd grew louder in response to this request and with that the Rev hit me in the forehead and I crashed to the ground and started flopping around like I had electrodes attached to my private parts. The crowd was cheering and the Rev said, "We'll come back and check on this young man when he regains his earthly senses," and down the line he went.

Well, of course, I hadn't been slain in the spirit and my back was no better or worse, but the Rev and I put on a great show. A minute or two later I got back to my feet, still playing the part, appearing a bit shaken, and as soon as the Rev saw me he was back with the microphone in my face.

"How does your back feel now? Is there any pain at all?"

"I never would have believed it, but the pain is gone! Thank you, thank you!" The crowd was cheering and the Rev was eating it up.

"Bend over and touch your toes!" the Rev commanded.

"I can do it! I can do it! Thank you, thank you!" (It may have been a miracle I could touch my toes after all the beer!)

After the show we waited backstage and as his "people" ushered him out to his custom tour bus (complete with whirlpool Jacuzzi) he spotted me and came over and shook my hand and said "Thanks, big man." It was my pleasure; although I'm not sold on his faith, you couldn't beat the performance.

The Reverends Benny and Sammy Hinn

Perhaps the Reverend Benny Hinn is more famous than his faith-healing brother Sammy, but both put on a great show of miracle cures, religious frenzies, music and "slaying people in the spirit," not only by the laying of hands, but also simply by breathing on them – either strong faith or bad breath, in my opinion. At one time both had their faith healing ministries in the Orlando area and as it happened, as I remember, both had children that skated in the youth hockey program at the ice rink that I happened to oversee as the General Manager of the recreation company that owned it.

One Saturday morning the manager of the rink called me to alert me that he felt the ice was not smooth enough for the youth hockey group to safely skate on. He told me there would be some upset parents and he would like me to be there to back up his decision not to allow skating on the bumpy ice that morning, strictly for safety reasons.

Upon arriving at the rink, a few parents were upset but most understood the reason for the cancellation was simply the safety of their children and we promised them we would get them other ice time that would work for all of them. Everyone seemed to accept what was a decision that was in their children's best interest and was not going to be reversed.

One parent, in particular, seemed intent on continuing the confrontation, yelling at me, saying I didn't know anything about ice safety and basically staying "in my face." I very rarely back down when confronted in this manner but the ice rink manager pulled me aside in mid-confrontation to alert me that the "gentleman" I was speaking with was the Rev. Sammy Hinn.

Going back to Rev. Hinn, he was happy to start in on me again, and never one to back down from a good argument we squared off again. After a minute or two more of his yelling I simply said "Rev. Hinn, I have a very simple solution; call upon the Heavenly Powers and go lay your hands on the ice and if you smooth the surface, I'll be happy to let the kids skate."

End of discussion, end of problem. Rev. Hinn was speechless and walked away and the youth hockey league went on from the next Saturday forward.

Jim and Tammy Faye Bakker

One of my favorite TV shows of all time was *The PTL Club* with Jim and Tammy Faye Bakker. I watched it knowing they were modern P.T. Barnums, yet I couldn't get enough of the show. I was honestly watching it as a comedy with Jim tying religion into timeshare pitches and Tammy's wonderful, tearful soliloquies with the black mascara running down her face. It amazed me that it took as long as it did for anyone to question when 20 million dollars is brought in and 19 million of it go to Jim and Tammy's living expenses, that there might be a problem.

When Jim Bakker was originally put in jail, Tammy announced she was moving the Jim and Tammy Faye Ministries to Orlando. With Jim incarcerated, you would think Tammy Faye might lie low, but like any other performer, she still craved the spotlight. During this time Tammy Faye lived in the very exclusive Orlando development of

Bay Hill and every Saturday morning visited a flea market where I owned a shop selling rock and roll tee shirts and memorabilia.

Almost every Saturday morning Tammy Faye would walk the flea market, in her public persona of wild outfits, tons of makeup and ham it up for all to see. She still loved playing the part even if it was a travesty of her former self. The outfit I remember most was a black spandex one piece body suit, skin tight with black boots, looking a bit bizarre on this aging, overweight little lady with the overly done face paint. But the "signature" of this outfit was a large gold sequined dollar sign ($) emblazoned on her chest like Superman's S. Wearing that took guts.

I always asked Tammy to take her picture with me but she always refused. She told me the reason was because I sold rock tee shirts and she knew some rock groups were satanic so she didn't want to. I'm not sure if selling rock music tee shirts is as bad as duping people out of life savings for unbuilt religious timeshares but... regardless, I would have loved a picture with this great entertainer.

I guess it wasn't all fun and games for Tammy Faye either. Once she was walking down the aisle where my shop was and was approached by a luggage dealer who had the shop across the way from me. Tammy was looking at his wares and he said "Tammy Faye, I have this great knock off of a Ralph Lauren briefcase, the real ones go for $2000 but I'll let you have this one for $200, $50 off the retail price." (Remember husband Jim has just entered jail for racqueteering.)

Tammy Faye examined it thoroughly, pronounced it a good copy saying "I don't want it but is a good copy and the reason I know is Jim has a real one."

The storeowner, a bit miffed I guess, said "Yeah, and a lot of good it's doing him now." Ouch!

ONE PAGE WONDER

After putting in my two-week notice at the Orange County Civic Center, the Security Director Tom Stark did all in his power to make me quit by giving me horrible jobs to do. One of the perceived worst was to take the wet 100,000 feet of fire hose from the building, fresh and soaked from the annual test and stretch it out on its edge in the expansive parking lot to dry during the heat of the day in August. Although I was promised help in the task, it rapidly became evident I was going to be doing this nasty hot heavy job alone. I decided I would not only complete the task but do so sending a message. Eight hours later, when looking out from the offices on the second floor to the parking lot, I had laid the white hose out on the black pavement, on its side as asked and in a space bigger than a football field in giant letters it read:

BEST WISHES

FRANK LYNCH

CHAPTER 7
KENNY ROGERS' TEE SHIRTS

I had the opportunity to work quite a few of Kenny Rogers' concerts in the early 1980s when he could sell out large venues and was truly a superstar of country music. The odd thing about that was he went out of his way to tell us that his show was not a "typical country music show." The backstage crew was reminded not to ask for pictures, autographs or engage in any discussion with Mr. Rogers unless he initiated it. I joking asked if we should look down at our shoe tops anytime he walked passed, and was answered by silence, as if maybe it wasn't such a bad idea.

We were also told of his unique way of greeting his fans. Kenny would not shake hands with ANYONE but during the first two songs of show did allow people to come down to the stage with gifts ranging from flowers to clothing to jewelry and Kenny would accept these gifts and drop them behind him in the "pit" where the band members were, as he played concerts in the round at this time. The irony of it all was Kenny never really kept anything, as soon as the show was over and Kenny had left the stage and the houselights came up, his band members would scramble for the forgotten gifts laying at their feet, flowers for the tour bus or wives of the local musicians, clothing and jewelry for themselves, just a perk of working the Kenny Rogers show.

Kenny's manager was Ken Kragen and he had at the beginning of Kenny's career once said "Stay with me and I will make you a millionaire." Years later, with the millions they had both made notwithstanding, Ken Kragen wrote Kenny Rogers a check for one million dollars to pay off his promise to him from those early days.

During the height of his popularity Kenny was scheduled to perform at the Orange County Convention Center in Orlando, I was the backstage manager and usually the liaison between the performer and his staff and the building staff. This was one of the times I wished I wasn't. The convention center's standard contract with performers included a provision that they send back a signed agreement on concession sales (tee shirts, etc.) four days before the show or the performer couldn't hawk his goods. Since Kenny's people hadn't sent the required paperwork in, building management assumed Kenny was not going to sell any merchandise and when his people started setting up the stands and were stopped, all hell broke loose. Ken Kragen demanded I take him to the management office where he was promptly told by the Asst. Director of the facility that because no contract had been signed, no shirts or programs could be sold. Ken offered to sign the contract on the spot and was told that wasn't good enough. When he then asked what he COULD do he was told he could possibly set up somewhere off property, outside the parking area and maybe sell there. With that Kragen took the performance contract, tore it into little pieces and tossed it in the Asst. Mgr.'s face saying "Then we aren't playing tonight."

The building manager said that was his decision but he would have to be the one to go out onstage and tell 14,000 Kenny Rogers fans that he would not appear. On purpose or unwittingly, she was calling his bluff and it worked. After the heated confrontation, Kenny appeared and no tee shirts were sold. And for whatever reason Ken Kragen, after that, always considered me as an ally and whenever Kenny played in Florida I usually got a call asking if I wanted to work the show. And even though officially they were "not available" I always got lots of Kenny Rogers merchandise and autographed photos as a thank you after the shows.

CHAPTER 8
VICTOR THE WRESTLING BEAR

As backstage manager for a Sports & Auto Show, I heard that among the attractions was Victor the Wrestling Bear. Being an animal lover and a wrestling fan I was intrigued by the concept. Although outlawed in many places today as cruelty to animals, the shows I saw were actually much more cruel to the people stupid enough to enter the ring against Victor than to the bear. Victor traveled with "The Original Gentle Ben" from the TV series of the same name. While I remain skeptical if he was the original, he certainly was old enough to be. Gentle Ben was lead into the arena, a giant sized old, old bear, made his way onstage where he promptly laid down and didn't move for the entirety of each appearance. As I remember the handlers charged for Polaroid pictures of folks with Gentle Ben.

As I stated Ben would just lay there motionless for his entire stay on stage which was 45 minutes at a time. Then each and EVERY time his handler would say "Time to go Ben", Ben would lumber up to all fours and pee. And when I say pee, I mean pee at least a gallon of foul liquid onstage.

But I digress, back to Victor... there are a few things anyone SHOULD know before wrestling a bear and it was blatantly obvious that no one who made the bad judgment to try knew any of those things. For instance a bear is 400 pounds of pure muscle easily at least 4 times as strong as any human. They also are at least three times as fast.

So no one could hurt Victor, they might anger him a bit (another bad idea) but certainly not hurt him. And a bear's natural instinct is take any of its prey off its feet so it appears in human terms as if he is "wrestling" I saw little men and big men, all of questionably sanity, all get manhandled (or is that bear handled?) by Victor. And it seemed the bigger they were the more delight Victor took in pulverizing them.

And perhaps most importantly, even if you live through the mauling, was another bear fact, whether wrestling a bear or just petting one, a bear has very oily fur. This is used in the wild to mark his territory from other bears. In captivity if you touch a bear, that foul smelling oil gets on you and remains on you for longer than any skunk spray would. So not only did people leave Victor's ring bruised, battered and a loser, but for at least a week everyone they came in contact with would be able to smell their encounter with my friend Victor the Wrestling Bear!

CHAPTER 9
BILLY JOEL'S PANTS & RANTS

When two Long Island boys like Billy Joel and I got together it was bound to be a memorable experience. His contract was the first I had ever dealt with that called for a seamstress to be on site for the show. In this case I certainly was glad she was there.

This was at the time when gossip columnists were first saying there might be a romance between Billy and Christine Brinkley, at that time one of the most beautiful women in the world. I was thinking he had to be the luckiest man alive as we were getting ready to walk to the stage that night. Once we were onstage Billy peeked out from behind the curtain and saw a bevy of beautiful women in the front row. He turned to me and said, "Wow look at those pretty ladies out there! If we don't have fun tonight something's wrong." I was kind of shocked and was about to say something like, "Hey, you've got Christie Brinkley, think about the rest of us," when suddenly the curtain went up and Billy bounded out on stage.

Billy hit the stage running and jumped up and slid across the top of his piano. Unbeknownst to either of us, this piano had a nail sticking up from it and as he slid across the piano, it tore a slice in his pants from his butt down past his knee. He realized before I did and came over to where I was standing in the wings, explained what happened to the audience, flashed them a bit and then wrapped the stage curtain around himself like a sarong and took off his pants and handed them to me to give to the seamstress. The audience of course was laughing and Billy charmed everyone with his off the cuff stories for the few minutes it took the seamstress to repair them. I found it all amazing that in all my years in the business, this was the only time a contract asked for a seamstress and the only time one was ever needed.

When I brought the pants back, I got a round of applause from the audience and held the curtain for Billy so he could put his repaired pants back on. With all that behind him, the Piano Man took to the stage for another one of his incredible shows.

Billy Joel & Author

CHAPTER 10
WILLIE NELSON'S MAGIC BUS

Over the years I had the privilege to work many Willie Nelson shows. They were always a lot of fun and everyone who had worked together before greeted each other like old friends. Willie's shows are usually advertised as Willie Nelson & Family and his shows certainly always had that kind of feel.

Back in the early 1980s you may remember the Barbara Walters specials on television. One of the most publicized of those shows was her one-on-one interview with Willie Nelson. Just prior to this interview there was a well-publicized medical study about the bad effects of smoking marijuana. Willie was coming on the Barbara Walters show to come clean about his past drug usage and make "an important announcement about his future."

On the show Willie admitted that he and most of his band members and road crew smoked pot! But he was there in front of Barbara, God and America to say there would no longer be drugs on his shows.

Two nights after this show aired, I was backstage working the Willie Nelson Show. I spotted Willie sitting by himself and went over and reintroduced myself and we started talking. I remember talking about Elvis with him among other things. At one point he asked me if I had seen his new bus yet. I said I hadn't. So he told me, "After you get me on stage, go take a look at the new bus, I'll tell them you're coming." So after he was onstage and things were under control I snuck out back to the new tour bus. The driver greeted me as if he knew me and we boarded the bus. He started showing me all the incredible features of the new bus. He said Willie especially liked the new bedroom and wanted me to see it. As we walked to the back of the bus, there was a kitchen type table on the right. Sitting on that table was what looked like at least a pound of marijuana!! The driver said "Don't mind that" when he saw me looking at it in disbelief after what I had heard just a few nights before on national television.

The bedroom was indeed spectacular with custom sculpted wood everywhere but I had to laugh at the drug discovery I had made. Looking back I think I put more faith in Willie and less in that medical study because here we are more than 25 years later and having just recently seen Willie again, he is alive and well and still putting on incredible shows.

Willie Nelson & Author

ONE PAGE WONDER

An interesting adage from the original Adventurers' Club at Pleasure Island:

Sometimes you get the bear,

sometimes the bear gets you,

BUT ALWAYS dress for the hunt.

CHAPTER 11
THE INCOMPARABLE HUGH SHANNON

One of the greatest performers and showmen that I ever worked with is someone you may never have heard of. He was a "saloon singer," was known as "The Pied Piper of the Jet Set", and his name was Hugh Shannon. Luckily just before his death a commercial video was made of one of his performances and it captures some of his uniqueness, but having spent two summers in his employ there are so many more stories to tell and a few will be related here. Many were lost with the man when he died, he had started an autobiography called *Let Him Play the Piano Dearie*, but sadly I don't think it was finished or it would have been a bestseller.

When Hugh Shannon came to The Bath & Tennis Club in Westhampton Beach, New York, in the summer of 1973 to headline in his own club, it was stated in his contract that a car and driver were to be at his call. I was working the front desk of the resort at that time and was told by the General Manager that I was to fill that position as well as my regular duties. The people I met, parties I attended and adventures I went on could be a book in itself.

Hugh Shannon started out by befriending the immortal Billie Holiday and it was she that told him that his piano playing and vocal styling were so unique that he should become an entertainer. Her famous quote upon hearing him sing at a party for Duke Ellington was "Man, you don't sound like nobody! You gotta sing!"

For years Hugh had clubs in all the famous playgrounds of the world, Cannes, Capri, Paris, London, the Hamptons and the people who came to hear him in these places read like a Who's Who of the Rich and Famous. Among those who I got to meet were Cary Grant, Dyan Cannon, Jackie Onassis, members of the Rockefellers, Vanderbilts, Whitneys, Kennedys, Guggenheims, the legendary Bricktop, Lionel Hampton, Mercer Ellington, Cy Coleman and many other stars and socialites too numerous to mention. Anyone who was anyone knew the place to see and be seen was at one of Hugh's shows.

Hugh's personality was as flamboyant as his stage character and was added to (or detracted from) by the gallon of white wine he drank each day during daylight hours and the Campari and sodas and straight vodkas in water glasses he drank each night during his shows.

As his driver and for much of the time the only person he saw who he knew each day, I became his confidant. This was great for me as I would bring my dates to his very chic and expensive club, be introduced like the "important" people and never pay for a thing.

On almost a daily basis when I was working he would call for a car saying he had an important appointment and I would be sent, while being paid by the resort, to drive him to his appointments. These "appointments" almost always were lunches at trendy restaurants, parties, socialite fundraisers etc., and I got to tag along and aside from being paid also never spent a dime!

I gave Hugh the sheet music for Scott Joplin's "The Entertainer" that was used as the theme for the movie *The Sting* and Billy Joel's "Piano Man" and he played both in his shows until his last day. Aside from Hugh the only other saloon singer I got to meet through him was Mr. Bobby Short and the two of them used to take turns as the stars at the famous El Morocco nightclub in New York City. I also introduced Hugh to Elvis Presley when Elvis appeared at Nassau Coliseum in New York. Hugh and I went to the show and I remember him being completely entranced and came back to his own club, telling everyone of his experience and giving one of the most inspired shows of his life.

Hugh's flamboyant personality coupled with his drinking led to many wild incidents. One of the wildest was when I got a call at home on a Saturday afternoon from the resort's General Manager saying that Hugh was running up and down the ocean beachfront stark naked, excepting an enormous American Indian war bonnet headdress with an eight foot trail of feathers down the back, whooping like a Banshee. You can imagine that might have taken the beachgoers a bit aback. When I arrived, indeed there was this naked inebriated "Indian" on the beachfront warpath. I told him he needed to put some clothes on and he said, "My dear boy, in Capri this would be a daily occurrence." He walked up to his room and I didn't see him again until show time when he went onstage and did his usual great show and the incident was never spoken of again until this writing.

One day I drove Hugh to the trendy Main Street shops of Westhampton Beach. In one store he saw a woven straw hat made in China and bought it. That night when I went up to his room to tell him it was fifteen minutes till show I saw the hat (purchased hours earlier) sitting on a chair. As a joke, I put the hat on and said, "Hugh, where did you get this great hat?"

Hugh replied, "Funny you should ask, my dear boy. On my trip to China last winter I met this elderly peasant woman weaving these hats on the side of the road in the frigid temperatures…" and he continued with a long elaborate story of his interactions with this old lady over the purchase of the hat. He told the story with such charm and emotion he almost had me believing he bought it 10,000 miles away rather than ten minutes away. When he finished his tall tale I simply said, "Hugh, I was with you when you bought this, this morning."

He looked at me for a second and said "So you were, my dear boy, so you were," and went on getting ready for his show as if nothing had happened. I'm not sure how many people he told the peasant woman story to, but it was all a part of his unique charm. Even if only ten percent of the stories he told me were true, he remains one of the most interesting people I ever met, who despite his questionable lifestyle was a devout Catholic and never missed Mass on Sundays.

To my knowledge Hugh's autobiography was never published. When I would ask him about it he would always say he was waiting for some famous people to die so he could tell the real truth about all the decadence he had witnessed and been a part of. Sadly, he died before the others.

If you are interested in listening to a saloon singer, check eBay for the VHS tape or DVD of one of Hugh Shannon's last performances. It isn't him at his peak, but it is a glimpse of a form of entertainment that no longer exists. Hugh died of throat cancer and it was suggested it was from all the decades of nights of singing, while the smoke from his cigarettes and the vodka ran across his inflamed vocal cords. He was truly one-of-a-kind.

Hugh Shannon

CHAPTER 12
ARE YOU READY FOR SOME FOOTBALL?

I love professional football and I have been lucky enough to be involved on various levels with the NFL, the World League and the USFL. A couple great sports stories follow...

At the time when I attended Biscayne College, it was the camp of the Miami Dolphins. We interacted with (and ate meals with) the Dolphins players every day during training camp and the season. Since we were with them all the time there really wasn't any hero worship, we got along with some players and didn't get along with others. Some of that stemmed from the fact our swimming pool was adjacent to their practice field and most days when classes were over it meant getting a cooler of beer, heading to the pool and berating the players from the safety of the other side of the chain link fence as they went through their practice.

Not many of them practicing in full pads in that scorching heat found us funny.

One day at lunch the team was all seated at one end of our cafeteria and we students at the other end. At our long rectangular tables I happened to be seated facing the team while friends of mine sitting across from me had their backs to them. One of my friends, Rick Berry was seated facing me so his back was to the team. He thought it would be funny to put a big glob of mashed potatoes on his spoon and laying it on his plate, hit the spoon, catapulting the mashed potatoes. When he did this, the potatoes flew over his shoulder heading towards the Miami Dolphins. I began to laugh, even harder when I saw them splat on a giant Dolphins defensive lineman. What I failed to realize was that with Rick's back to them, the team didn't know where the potatoes came from. However when they looked up all they saw was me laughing hysterically in their faces and they assumed en masse that I must have thrown them.

They descended on me and I saw my life flash before my eyes. Luckily I talked my way out of it by showing that (thank God) I didn't have mashed potatoes and was truly just laughing at something else at the time. Thanks Rick!

My being at Biscayne led the NFL to hire me as security for Super Bowl XIII. The Pittsburgh Steelers practiced at our school and we basically hung out watching them, checking credentials of those watching. It was obviously much more lax than it is today. Once game day arrived I was told I would be working on-field security. While others paid hundreds for a ticket to the Super Bowl there I was in the corner of the end zone, being paid with the best seat in the house. Prior to kickoff as I looked into the stands I saw Danny Jiggetts of the Chicago Bears walking by. I had gone to high school with Danny and yelled to him. He came down and said "What are you doing down there and I have to sit up here?" I told him the NFL was paying me to protect people like him. We both had a good laugh and it was good to see him again. My face went down in history and anytime the highlights of Super Bowl XIII come on ESPN, when Lynn Swan makes his tremendous catch in the end zone, that's me front and center that he catches it right in front of. I think I have about 5 good appearances on that half-hour highlight reel.

The Orlando Renegades with then Head Coach, now famous TV sports analyst, Lee Corso were Central Florida's entry in the USFL. They played in the Tangerine Bowl in downtown Orlando. Working security for them was always fun especially with Coach Corso.

Once during a practice Coach Corso decided he would make the lunch run for the team for the day. Working security for him I was nearby as he shouted, "Anyone else need a sub sandwich? I am on my way." I shouted back, "I'll take a ham and cheese!" Coach looked over at me and said, "From the looks of things you've had a few too many sandwiches as it is," winked and walked off. I never got my sandwich.

Working the entrance tunnel to the field from the locker room one night for a televised USFL game, as the team was introduced and ran onto the field en masse, Coach Corso looked up and yelled, "Look at that full moon, great night for football!" One of the first players behind me looks at me and says "We've got a game to play and he's giving a weather report!" Ahhh, I miss the USFL.

Another TV game had me standing near the Renegades goalpost as they did their end zone sprints to warm up. I noticed one giant defensive lineman who was walking through it rather than running, so each time it was his turn I was saying things like, "Come on, push it, we've got a game to play!" This went on for his next four or five sprints. On his next turn as I started with my vocal "encouragement" not only did he run the ten yards at full speed but never breaking stride continued and ran right over me, planting me in the turf. I was seeing stars and he had a big smile on his face. I didn't say anything after that. I really don't miss the USFL.

A third Renegades game had me patrolling the sidelines and I kept noticing this drunk, wild-eyed hillbilly type in the lower stands waving a large rebel flag. Shortly before halftime he made his way down to the front row of seats and catching my attention told me he was going to run across the field at half.

I told the drunken rebel to enjoy himself in the stands, but that he wasn't allowed on the field and it wasn't worth getting arrested over. I lost track of him for a while, but as halftime drew to a close and the players were coming back on the field, I turned to my right and who is running down the sidelines on the field but my "pal" with the rebel flag. He was so intent on his moment of glory he never saw me coming. I ran at him full speed as he ran at me, and like two locomotives hitting head on I planted him about 5 yards back and into the turf. He was knocked out, the police hauled him off, the crowd cheered, and the players were all congratulating me on my "hit." The Renegades went on to lose the game by thirty points and in the Orlando Sentinel paper the next day, bemoaning the loss, it read "the best tackle of the night for Orlando was made by Frank Lynch, who works sideline security for the team when he made a vicious open field tackle on a trespassing fan during halftime." Ahhh, I do miss the USFL.

Years later I ran into Coach Corso in an office supply store and went up to say hello. I didn't expect him to remember me and he didn't. When I said "Hi, Coach!" in typical Corso fashion he grabbed me in a playful headlock and said, "How's it going big guy?" and looked down at my shirt which happened to have a New York Mets logo on it. "How's those Mets doing? Good to see you," and walked off. It didn't matter to Coach Corso that it was December and there was no baseball, nor did it to me, for that was Coach Corso and I was glad to have run into him again. I DO miss the USFL!

CHAPTER 13
THE GODFATHER OF SOUL

"Ladies and gentleman, the Godfather of Soul, the hardest working man in America today, Mr. James Brown!" So goes a small part of the introduction for an American original, James Brown. He is in that exclusive class of music pioneers with Elvis, Bo Diddley and only a few others who shaped what music was to become. I was lucky enough to spend the better part of two days just sitting and talking with Mr. Brown and then working the stage for one of his legendary performances.

Assigned as his personal bodyguard for the Budweiser sponsored Black Music Festival in Miami, the show was supposed to be on Saturday night but rain postponed the show until Sunday night. So Mr. Brown and I sat in his dressing room trailer for about 30 of the 48 hours of those two days, much of the time alone. Once I got used to his accent, or would it be dialect, we actually had long conversations on a variety of subjects and I found him very intelligent and well-versed. I remember he had at least 100 stage outfits with him, each embroidered with the letters "JB" even though rather obviously he was only going to wear one on stage. I also remember being struck by how short and slight he was in stature and yet onstage while performing he seemed like a giant, a sign of a legendary performer.

One interesting quirk about my time with the Godfather of Soul was that after spending hours with him, when the makeup artist came in just prior to show time, Mr. Brown asked me to wait outside the trailer. At first I thought he was kidding but he was serious. So each of the two days when the makeup artist arrived I went and stood outside the door for the few minutes it took for his makeup to be applied, his stage outfit put on and then I returned to the dressing room ready to walk him to the stage.

As I had mentioned the show was scheduled for Saturday night, but rain postponed the show until Sunday. With the show going on Sunday night, James Brown was the headliner and final act of the night. During his show, the Miami Police liaison for the show came up to me and said, "Get him off the stage now!" Unbeknownst to us, there was a Sunday night noise ordinance in Miami (10 PM) and the show had to be stopped as it was 10:01.Of course with 30,000 fans grooving to the beat had I just walked onstage and taken Mr. Brown off, a riot most likely would have ensued. Luckily just as he ended a song Mr. Brown came to side stage to get a drink of water, we whisked him back to the dressing room, explaining the situation as we went, the emcee thanked the crowd for coming and they dispersed none the wiser.

Later in my career I had to remove Hank Williams Jr. from the stage in the same situation, but that turned out to not be as easy.

We lost James Brown on Christmas Day 2006. He will never be forgotten or replaced. He was a true American original.

ONE PAGE WONDER

At the informational meeting for the graduating seniors of Biscayne College Class of 1977, a college professor stated, "Graduation caps and gowns can be picked up in the school library starting tomorrow. Are there any questions?"

My good friend Justin Barrett raised his hand and asked, "Yeah. Where is the library?"

CHAPTER 14
MONKEY BUSINESS

I was an organ grinder. Although most of you don't know what that means, not only was I one, but it was also one of my most rewarding jobs both financially and emotionally. I will explain that in detail in a bit but suffice to say for now it involves monkeys and my fascination with primates (monkeys and apes) goes way back.

This fascination started back in 1968 when I attended a pet show and saw a two-year-old chimpanzee named Tuff Guy and his owner Vicki Ardito. The chimp was riding a tricycle, playing with his toys, pretty much oblivious to the crowd around him. I think I stood watching him for 5 or six hours, entranced and knew I wanted one.

Luckily, I did some research and realized a chimp was not the greatest pet choice. Number one they grow up to be incredibly strong, sometimes vicious, animals that in most cases were then either turned over to zoos or euthanized. Secondly a baby chimp in 1968 sold for about $750, much more money than I as a thirteen-year-old had ever even seen at one time. (Today a baby chimp sells for around $50,000. Talk about inflation!) I eventually purchased my first monkey, a baby male golden spider monkey named Melvin, for $60, including the cage. Today, that same monkey would be at least $7000 to buy.

Over the years, I never missed a chance to visit any place that had monkeys, be it a promotional appearance, a circus, a zoo, a pet shop or someone's backyard. I collected books on monkeys (if you want to see what we go through read the book *He's Not a Monkey, He's an Ape and He's Our Son!*), joined the Simian Society of America, and became friends with "monkey people." People like the late Lenny Schendowich, "The Monkey's Uncle," who worked monkeys out of Miami and the great chimpanzee trainer and photographer Gini Valbuena, who over the last 20 years has been responsible for not only the pictures on our famous Christmas cards, but also has given me the opportunity to work with chimps, orangutans, bobcats and other animals at her compound. Two great "monkey people" friends!

In 1985, I saw an ad for squirrel monkeys in Amusement Business magazine. Thinking having a troop of six squirrel monkeys might be fun, I ordered them. My brother-in-law Joe Murphy and I set out building a large cage to house the monks when they arrived. We were so diligent in our task we built a cage so large it couldn't fit through the door into the house where it was to be placed. Needless to say, we had to cut a portion of the cage away just to get it inside. It should have been a forewarning of what was to come next.

My dear wife Barbara, at that time, was in charge of the Winter Park Junior High School flag corps and they were to be having a dinner party at our house. As luck would have it that dinner party was scheduled on the same day as the unexpected arrival of the new baby squirrel monkeys.

When I got the call the monkeys were waiting for me at the airport, I raced to pick them up. I brought them home, took them out of their shipping crate and put them in their new cage. Scared and befuddled, they huddled together and were nowhere near as excitable and frantic as squirrel monkeys can be.

Not long thereafter, the guests started arriving for the dinner party and thought it so cute that they would be eating a formal sit down dinner next to a cage of cute baby monkeys. That thought only lasted until the young ladies were all seated at the table and a large bowl of pasta was presented. As cage builders, we had not taken into account how tiny baby squirrel monkeys are and used 2-inch chicken wire as the cage "bars." As soon as the monkeys saw the pasta as food, they all came charging right through the 2-inch holes, dove onto and across the now-screaming teenagers and into the spaghetti. Monkeys and teenagers were jumping everywhere, pasta was flying and the once again frightened monkeys took off on a rampage around the house, racing across curtain rods, swinging from drapes... well, you get the picture. That is if you are picturing six scared frantic monkeys, eight terrified teens, an angry wife and me.

Catching the monkeys at this point proved to be of no use as once I would catch one and put him in the cage, he would just squeeze out again. I raced to the hardware store, bought 1-inch chicken wire, returned and wrapped the cage in it. The formal dinner party then became a safari as we chased, herded and caught all the monkeys and returned them to their now inescapable cage.

Not having learned my lesson, one fateful day in October 1989, while reading through Circus Report magazine, I came upon an ad for two fully trained, ready-to-perform organ grinder monkeys (capuchin monkeys). I knew I had to have them. I contacted the owner in Texas and he drove the animals to Orlando. He, not knowing of my background with primates, told me he fed them fried chicken, table scraps, etc. I was horrified to think that might be true, as primates have a very strict diet that does not include fried foods. The owner himself was a bit odd as well. He told me he was selling the monkeys because he was moving to Japan to take a long term engagement as a female impersonator. Now I am not sure what Japanese tastes are in their women (or women wannabes), but this guy was no taller than 5' 4" and had to weigh over 400 pounds! He was wider than he was tall and the image of him dressed as a woman scares me to this day. Undaunted by his appearance or bizarre story and worried about the welfare of the two monkeys, I bought the pair on the spot for $9500.

Bea Bea and Ko Ko were two great monkeys and we spent the next five years working together. All the memorable moments we had together could fill a book on their own (and may one day) but a few of their hijinks will be reported here.

Bea Bea was a weeper capuchin and Ko Ko was a cinnamon ringtail capuchin. Bea Bea had dark black fur and Ko Ko's was an almost silver color. Although they looked completely different and had completely different personalities, they loved being together and when I would take one to work, if the other wasn't going she would hoot and cry and make a fuss until we were out of sight.

Both monkeys came to me with full wardrobes, but Bea Bea always preferred her red, white and blue patriotic overalls, so much so that I had six more pairs made exactly the same. Aside from getting dressed, both monkeys had been taught to take coins from people, put the coin in their pocket, then shake hands. Bea Bea would also take a dollar bill, bring it to me, and in exchange I would give her a souvenir picture (of herself of course) which she would then hand to whoever gave her the dollar. Amazingly, even in large crowds she always gave the picture to the same person who gave her the dollar bill. She was quite remarkable.

Ko Ko on the other hand wore pants, a vest and a hat and didn't particularly like getting dressed. Once dressed, she was fine, but she would always squirm while being dressed. Ko Ko could pocket coins but unlike Bea Bea who seemed to know the purpose of it, Ko Ko would become bored and after awhile, throw the coins, or want to just play with the customers. While Bea Bea shook hands, Ko Ko loved to give kisses and if I said, "Give a kiss," Ko Ko would. If the person happened to be standing straight up and not bent over interacting with her, she would leap straight up in the air, plant a kiss on their face, and drop back to the ground. It was a crowd-pleaser for sure.

We spent over four years appearing nightly at the Church Street Market in downtown Orlando, back when that area was a tourist destination. We never used an actual organ or music maker in our show because the crowds were always so large. In the old days, the organ was used to drum up the crowd, hence the term organ grinder meaning a man, his organ and a monkey who takes money from the customers.

Our pitch was always the same. I had Bea Bea on a six foot lead and would say "If you'd like to meet the monkey, give her a quarter and she will shake your hand, give her a dollar and she'll shake your hand and bring you her personal photo and hand it to you herself." A circle of people would form around us and off we would go, working the circle left to right, because as it turned out both Bea Bea and I are left handed!

Bea Bea was trained to take a coin and put it in her pocket. A touch to her lead from me and that was her signal to move on without shaking hands. When we asked for a quarter for a handshake, thousands of times I was asked, as some cheapskate held out a dime, "Does she know the difference between a dime and a quarter?" Bea Bea would take the dime, I'd tap her leash and she'd move on, seemingly "knowing" the difference and not shaking hands with the customer. The customer would almost always then hold out a quarter, Bea Bea would take it and shake hands and the customer would say, "Wow! She really is smart!"

My answer was always the same and always produced a loud laugh from the crowd. "Sir, it's not that she is so smart, it's just that you aren't so smart, because you just paid 35 cents for a handshake that cost everyone else a quarter!"

Of course we made much more money from the folks who gave Bea Bea a dollar for her preprinted photo. In order to increase the number of dollar-givers we worked up a great routine for the early evenings when there were large numbers of families in attendance. My daughter Shannon was a toddler at the time and she and my wife would come down to our show. When all the kids were crowded around with their quarters out and parents standing right behind them, Shannon would hold out a dollar bill. Bea Bea, seeing her "sister" would race over, start to play with her a bit, take the dollar, bring it to me and then I'd give her the photo to take back to Shannon. She'd hand it to Shannon, hug her, and kiss her until I would say "Wow! Bea Bea likes you," and have Bea Bea move on. Of course no one knew it was my own daughter who had been raised with Bea Bea. Immediately, every single child in that circle turned around to their parent, handed back their quarter and demanded a dollar bill to give to Bea Bea. It was a moneymaker and Shannon's launch into show business. My wife Barbara would then take Shannon for a walk and come back every ten minutes or so as a new crowd formed and we'd repeat the process over and over!

One late Saturday night a lady and a young girl approached us as we were working. I remember thinking it was neither the time nor place for such a young child to be. I watched as the lady reached into her bag and gave the girl a piece of paper that I could readily see was not a dollar bill. The young girl gave Bea Bea the piece of paper and Bea Bea stuffed it in her overalls pocket. Bea Bea shook hands with the child and moved on. The lady began yelling in a deep accent "What about the picture? What about the picture?" Having had our share of weirdoes who had tried to hand Bea Bea everything from cigarettes to play money, I explained that it had to be a dollar bill to receive the picture. The lady and child walked away. Later I reached into Bea Bea's pocket to remove the coins she had collected and the mysterious piece of paper.

The piece of paper was a US one dollar welfare food stamp. To this day I regret not giving that little girl a photo, but balance my regret with wonder as to why the little girl was there at 11 p.m., why someone would give up a food stamp and my personal dislike for the food stamp program in general.

On the flip side, Bea Bea and Ko Ko developed quite a following of regulars, people who night after night stopped by, and gave them their change or a dollar just to get their handshake and a few moments with these remarkable animals. One of the most heartwarming stories was of a family consisting of a father, mother and two young daughters. I saw a man running through the area towards us shouting "There she is! There she is! There's Bea Bea!" The mother and two daughters followed and were soon up front handing Bea Bea dollar after dollar. The father came to my side and said "Thank God you are here. Last year my girls each gave Bea Bea a dollar and got her picture. Those pictures have been on our refrigerator ever since. We live in Milwaukee and all the way down on the plane yesterday, when we tried to tell the girls about Disney World, Mickey, Sea World, Universal and all the rest, all they would say was 'I hope Bea Bea is still there.' This is the highlight of their vacation."

I, of course, took them aside and let them play with Bea Bea, get some pictures taken with her, etc., and it made me proud to be doing what we were.

Then there were also my imposters who gave both me and what I did a bad name. They would occasionally show up in the general area and try and steal my business. One example was two men who showed up with a pitiful little capuchin monkey chained to a table where it was forced to perform the same "trick" over and over. People were then asked to donate money, but could not get near the aggressive monkey. Horrible. Another time a lady showed with two monkeys. One was secured in a baby carriage and the other was taught to push it. Again there was no interaction and people were actually told to throw their donations in the direction of the carriage. Horrible as well. What Bea Bea and Ko Ko and I did was so different, we entertained and people got to interact with these two amazing animals and hopefully some kids became interested in monkeys from their visit with us as I had been years before with Tuff Guy the chimp.

I must say something here about the overzealous animal rights activists. We had our share of them and I always handled them the same way. While others might just walk away, I would suggest to them they take up a more pressing cause like the homeless in Orlando. I would remind them that these monkeys were a part of my family, born and raised in captivity, had the best of care and that I was strictly licensed to have them. When they suggested, as they always did, that I "let them go," I reminded them they had never seen a jungle, wouldn't like it if they did, and certainly couldn't survive in one.

Granted there are people who shouldn't have monkeys or exotic animals in their care, but there are many more people who shouldn't have children in their care and do. Being strictly licensed by both the state and federal government to keep monkeys I suggest the same overseeing should be done to parents to help stop child neglect and abuse. Animal rights people, focus your energy on a cause that can help humanity!

Aside from our nightly appearances at Church Street we appeared at many hotels, in the Citrus Bowl Parade, at many schools where I gave talks on monkeys and them NOT making good pets, charity events, fairs, festivals and conventions. After five years of organ grinding, I made the mistake of thinking I might need a "real" job and I sold the monkeys to a wonderful lady who owns the Appalachian Pet Farm in Pennsylvania. It truly was like selling my own children, but I knew they were going to great place where they would get lots of attention, as they were used to. If you are ever in the area stop by and visit the farm and say hi to them. And I am making no promises that I might not one day train Bea Bea's successor and start organ grinding all over again.

Thank You!
Your Friend Forever **Bea Bea**

CHAPTER 15
BIG BILLY Q

    Big Billy Q is not a celebrity. He is a good friend of mine who has worked backstage at many more shows than I have as he continued to work shows long after I "retired." He and I worked many shows side by side and there are many wild stories about our goings on. Bill always took things a bit more seriously than I did, so he would get in situations I wouldn't, but he was always fun to watch. Bill stands about 6'5" and weighs probably 350 pounds, so he is not a little guy. And he could have a short temper.

    Billy and I were working a Jimmy Buffet concert and decided after the show that the backstage staff should all go out for drinks and food. Once the show was over, about fifteen of us headed out to a restaurant close to the arena for a few cocktails and a bite to eat. Our group was seated on the second floor of the bar, which opened down to the first floor. We were seated at a large table in the middle of the second floor, with Billy at one end of the table and me at the other. Two couples were seated next to us, with our group on one side and the fifteen foot drop to the ground floor on their other side. These two couples had been at the show and had already had a few drinks. As the waitress came around taking our orders, the two couples were singing Jimmy songs rather loudly.

When the waitress got to Billy, he gave in his rather sizeable order and she said he needed to repeat it because she couldn't hear him over the singing. Billy said to the two couples, "Quiet down! I am trying to place an order here!" One of the ladies in the foursome yelled back, "You don't need any food, fat boy!" and Billy stood up. With that, all four people at their table jumped on Billy and started pummeling him.

Being at the far end of the table, I found it a bit amusing, assuming that the other guys at the table would stand up, break it up and it would end there. I guess because Billy was more than holding his own, amazingly they all just sat there and watched, laughing. Knowing the restaurant wouldn't put up with this for long, I came, from the far end of our table, to Billy's aid. As I slid past the other backstage workers, one couple was on their butts and done with the fracas. As I reached the now two-on-one battle, the girl was punching Billy in the back. Billy had her boyfriend by the neck and was holding him over the balcony threatening to drop him on the diners below. I told the girl to back off and she responded by slamming her high heel into the instep of my foot. Now that really hurt!

The problem was settled and everyone ended up okay... until years later when I had some foot problems and my doctor, looking at my foot x-ray, said "When did you break your foot here?" pointing to my instep. I said I didn't know I had, but thinking back it happened that night with Billy Q.

Twice in my concert career I have been told to go onstage and stop a performer in mid-concert. Once was with the Godfather of Soul, James Brown and the other was with Hank Williams Jr. at a show on his birthday. We had reached the 11PM curfew the City of Orlando had on concert noise and Hank was showing no signs of stopping. His manager Merle Kilgore pulled me aside and said "The only way we get him off is for me to call him over and you throw a blanket over him and hold him until he gets the idea the show is over." And that is exactly what we did!

Opening Hank's show was my buddy David Allan Coe. I was having a great time backstage saying hello to all my old friends and playing with David Allan's pet cougar. I went to the front of the stage to see how things were going with this very rowdy, beer drinking crowd. This was in a football stadium with the stage at one end and then the crowd on the field. At the far end of the stadium was a flag pole. A group of fans climbed up the pole a few feet and attached a rebel flag to the pole's rope and hoisted up the flag. Billy Q. was in the barricade between the stage and the crowd and I watched as he climbed over the barricade, pushed his way through the crowd to the far end of the stadium and took the flag down, handing back to its owners. The crowd booed as he came back through them and jumped over the barricade to the stage. No sooner had he gotten back than up went the flag again! Again he jumped over the barricade, back through the angry crowd, took the flag down, and returned it to its owners. Back through the crowd, back in the barricade, and up goes the flag again. Billy was livid and ready to take on the whole audience to get back and take the flag down again. I think a riot would have ensued. Luckily, just as he was about to enter the crowd again, David Allan Coe took the stage and Bill's attention had to turn to the event at hand. I remember shortly thereafter, a fight broke out in the crowd and David Allan Coe stopped his song and said, "This fight is more entertaining than anything I can do. I'll start once you guys finish." That stopped the fight and the rest of the night went on without incident.

I was backstage manager at a show featuring the band 38 Special, a great Southern rock band led by front man Donnie Van Zant whose brother Johnny is, of course, front man for Lynyrd Skynyrd. Billy Q was in the barricade directly in front of Donnie's microphone stand, with Donnie behind him and the crowd in front of him. Now Billy is a great guy to have in the barricade to keep things orderly and knows to keep his eyes on the audience, not the band. So when Donnie came onstage drinking a beer, Billy did not know it. When Donnie finished the beer, he tossed it in the crowd right in front of Billy. Billy saw none of that, but a few seconds later did see a guy in the crowd with a beer, not knowing it was the souvenir Donnie threw in the crowd. Since drinking wasn't allowed, Billy went after the guy with the beer, trying to take the can away. The guy and his friends took exception and started beating on Billy. I jumped out and got him back in the barricade. As I was trying to explain to him it was okay, Donnie started beating him over the head with his microphone stand from the stage! Luckily everything was cleared up quickly and the show went on without incident.

Billy is a great friend of mine and I hope he doesn't mind me sharing these stories. Keep in mind he and I have worked hundreds of shows and he is great at what he does. I wouldn't want anyone else to have my back. He has pulled injured people from crowds, broken up fights, protected band members and protected me. So the three humorous stories above are more than outweighed by the hundreds of shows that went on safe and secure because of Billy Q's work. He is a great guy.

Another pearl of wisdom from legendary coach and Professor Dr. Demie Mainieri:

"Boys, ALWAYS wear sunglasses to board meetings. That way if you are bored you can close your eyes and doze off and no one knows. On the other hand, if you want to make an impressive point during the meeting, start your presentation by giving it one of these shots." (He removes his sunglasses and looks around the room.) "It's very dramatic and they know you mean business!"

CHAPTER 16
PATTI WHO?

While writing this book, veteran punk rocker Patti Smith was awarded France's most prestigious arts award for her contribution to the music industry and inducted into the Rock & Roll Hall of Fame. When she released her first album "Horses" back in 1975, she was considerably less well-known and toured as an opening act for various tours.

One day back in late 1975 while getting ready for a concert, I looked out over the backstage area and saw a young lady sitting in the grass in a restricted area. I assumed she was just another misguided concertgoer who had wandered into this off-limits area. As I approached her she was gazing at the sky and commented, "Look at that beautiful sunset, isn't that something?" I agreed with her and told her that no matter how pretty it was, she wasn't allowed backstage and would have to leave. As I helped her up she said "But I'm here for the Patti Smith show."

I countered as I took her arm and started walking her out the backstage gate to the public parking area, "It's nice to know she has such loyal fans, but you still have to go."

"But you don't understand!" she continued.

"I understand you have to leave!" I retorted, grasping her arm a bit tighter in case she decided to make a run for the backstage dressing room area.

Suddenly, she started laughing hysterically and as I braced for the worst, she said, "Wait a minute, you really don't understand, I AM Patti Smith!"

Since she had no backstage pass on, I walked her back up to her dressing room area and verified that she was indeed THE Patti Smith, and took her backstage pass lanyard, put it around her neck, and told her to have a great show.

A few shows later it was reported she had fallen off a stage and broken her neck, ending her touring schedule for that year.

Who knew that many years later that unrecognizable face of a woman now nearing 60 years olds would receive the French government's top entertainment honor of the Commander of the Order of the Arts and Letters as a pioneer in punk rock music and be inducted in the Rock and Roll Hall of Fame. Congratulations, Patti!

CHAPTER 17
MR. CARY GRANT

As I have alluded to in the introduction to this book, I was always amazed at the people who could move an audience simply with their presence. One of the strangest examples of this was an incident I witnessed involving Cary Grant.

In July of 1972, I was working the front desk of the famed Bath & Tennis Club resort in Westhampton Beach. Mr. Grant and actress Dyan Cannon were divorced by his time, but still close friends and shared in raising their daughter, Jennifer. Ms. Cannon and Jennifer were staying at the resort and Mr. Grant would pop in, both to see them and catch Hugh Shannon's show at the resort. (See the Hugh Shannon chapter elsewhere in this book.)

This particular night, I was working the front desk of the resort alone and two middle-age ladies were checking in. I saw the lobby doors open and saw Mr. Grant enter and he walked through the lobby up the stairs to where the rooms were.

I said, "Good evening, Mr. Grant," and he replied, "Good evening Frank, how are you tonight?" in that famous voice of his, as he made his way to the stairwell.

Both ladies, who were facing me with their backs to Mr. Grant, spun around just in time to catch a glimpse of him as he went up the stairs. One of the ladies said, "Oh my God, that's Cary Grant!" and fainted dead away! Luckily, her friend caught her before she completely collapsed to the floor. Being that the entire lobby was done in marble, the lady could have been seriously hurt had she hit her head either on the front desk counter or the floor. She came to rather quickly and was rather embarrassed, but was okay.

So when people talk about stage presence or star power I always remember this incident when simply seeing Cary Grant caused a lady to pass out cold.

CHAPTER 18
THE BOB BARKER PARTY

The staff members at the Convention Center, myself included, were anxiously awaiting 5 p.m. on Friday to go home. We had all been at the Convention Center, some even sleeping there, for about 20 hours per day for the previous two weeks without a break. Two conventions and three concerts had stretched everyone to their limit and everyone was watching the clock on Friday as we actually had nothing scheduled for almost 24 hours! We wanted to go home.

We knew we had to be back at 5pm on Saturday for a sold-out show called "Bob Barker's Fun & Games Show." This was a live arena show featuring Bob Barker, in which he gave away prizes much like on his popular TV show, *The Price Is Right*.

But at 4:30 p.m. on Friday, the day before the show, all we had on our minds was leaving this building that we had spent almost every hour in for the past two weeks.

Suddenly an announcement came over the speaker system at the center, "There will be a MANDATORY all staff meeting in room six in 15 minutes." Everyone was shocked; you could almost hear the entire staff say at once, "WHAT????" at the end of the announcement. All we wanted was to go home. People went from office to office asking, "What is this about? Are they crazy? I want to go home. I haven't seen my kids in days!" etc.

Since we knew mandatory meant mandatory a large group of angry Center employees headed down to meeting room six. Upon opening the door to the meeting room, everyone was greeted with an incredible array of food and drink, a thank you from the building for all we had gone through. Salads, shrimp, roast beef – a true buffet of food – plus beer, wine, and soft drinks. Having survived on fast food for two weeks, everyone dove into the food. Of course with many of us having averaged a very few scant hours per night, everyone was also very overtired. But with free beer and wine and it being Friday afternoon, it wasn't very long until many of the attendees were not only stuffed with food, but most tipsy and a few downright drunk. The party had become loud and a bit raucous, and at first no one noticed as a door opened and a gentleman walked in. The partying continued, but one by one people fell silent as they noticed the man who had entered the party. Within a minute the group of about 100 fell silent with Bob Barker unexpectedly standing in the middle of the tipsy chaos.

So here stands TV icon Bob Barker looking at the entire staff that was to run his show the next night and most of the staff had already had far too much to drink. He surveyed the situation and said, "I came in to see the arena for the show tomorrow and asked someone where I might get a drink. They directed me here, but I had no idea that the drinks were so obviously available." With the tension broken, everyone started to laugh as one staffer poured Bob a glass of white wine.

The party quieted down a bit and I felt a bit sorry for Mr. Barker, standing there by himself with everyone staring at him. I walked up to him and told him I had been a fan of his since his days on the TV show *Truth or Consequences*. He said I was too young to remember that and I amazed him by recanting some of my favorite parts of the show. He and I sat and talked for probably an hour about Rosie Beaird the great girl pitcher of the Queen and Her Maids softball team and how they tricked Little Leaguers into batting against her, the surprise family reunions they staged, about performing animals, and it was great fun for both of us, I think.

The female staffer who had poured him his wine came over with the empty wine bottle and asked him if he would autograph it. I thought he showed a great sense of humor in signing "Rita, I'll never forget our night together, Bob Barker." What a great piece of memorabilia she has!

Although I doubt Mr. Barker knew about it, his show, although sold-out, was not very well received and he toured with it for only a short time. Why? There was a big difference between his TV show and the live show. At the live show, 8,000 people had paid $15 each hoping to win a car or another big prize. At the TV show the people are admitted free, so when they don't win, nothing is lost. Of the 8,000 people at our show, maybe 30 won prizes and by the time they were doing the drawing for the car, people were leaving saying what a rip off it was because they hadn't won anything and had paid $15 to win.

Bob Barker & Author

ONE PAGE WONDER

The hardest lesson I have learned in life, being a completely trusting person is that not all people are nearly as honorable. People who seem friendly and normal can be as psychotic and hurtful as any of the most notorious criminals. I guess my message to others would be, as the sergeants on the TV show *COPS* always say, "Be careful out there."

CHAPTER 19
KISS UNMASKED

The rock band KISS is legendary. It amazed me in the 1990s, when they had discarded their makeup and spectacle that they were still out touring, but only playing to small crowds. I kept telling people if they wanted to return to filling up arenas they needed to put the makeup back on and do the incredible stage shows they were known for.

I doubt my observations ever reached them, but someone must have suggested it and back in form they are again selling out arenas, as I write, on what has to be the world's longest farewell tour.

However, back in the day, KISS was very methodical in not allowing anyone to see them out of makeup. The afternoon of an evening KISS concert at the Hollywood Sportatorium I happened to walk onto the stage during what seemed to be a normal sound check.

As I walked up the stairs to the stage, two burly gentlemen grabbed me and put what felt like a blanket over my head and carried me back out the backstage door to the dressing room area.

I, of course, wasn't very happy and wondered what was going on. As it turned out I "almost was one of the first people" to see KISS without their makeup. I was never quite sure what the big deal was. I think many people had seen KISS without the greasepaint in their less famous days and not being a big fan I wouldn't have known if it were the guys of KISS or just the sound techs doing an instrument check had such a big deal not been made of it all.

The guys of KISS are among the richest entertainers out there between concerts, recordings, merchandise and the longevity of the band. A few years ago KISS front man Gene Simmons had a "reality" TV show called *Rock School*, where he teaches children to be rock stars. He tells them it isn't about singing talent or great instrumentation, but all about attitude. It is that attitude that has kept KISS going all these years and through it all their anthem rings true... "I wanna rock and roll all night and party every day!"

Author & Ken Osmond "Eddie Haskell"

Frankie Avalon & Author

George Jones & Author

CHAPTER 20
THE BANKED TRACK

As a child I did learn to roller skate and occasionally visited the local roller rink, but was never a great skater nor did I ever think it would factor into my later life. But even as a child, my fascination with pro wrestling did spill over into the then popular Roller Derby and the New York team, the New York Chiefs. Roller Derby, for those of you born after 1970, was like pro wrestling on roller skates, a great sports-entertainment package that toured with teams like the Midwest Pioneers, the Southern Outlaws and perhaps the most famous Bay Area Bombers from California.

The New York Chiefs were skating at Southampton College on Long Island in 1972 when I went to see them. As a junior in high school I had a great time yelling at the players, cheering on the home team and booing the "heels" (bad guys). After the match an older man, who I later found out was named Lou Donavon, walked up to me and asked me, "Do you think you could do that?" I replied, "Of course." He retorted, "If you can skate half as well as you can mouth, you could be a star in this league. Come see me," and gave me his card.

That card was for a roller derby training school based in Connecticut and I started driving the hour and a half each way at least twice a week to learn how to skate on the banked track. That training was not only on how to skate, but also on how to fight, fall, pull a punch and the rest. It was tough, but I enjoyed it. I certainly was not a great or even good skater, but I think Donavan remembered my mouth and delight in riling people up and so he kept me around.

The New York Chiefs were scheduled to skate at the Nassau Coliseum on Long Island. A bunch of us were invited and I was told, "Bring your skates, just in case." I was thrilled! Was I going to become a professional skater with the New York Chiefs? So excited in fact, I remember two things about getting there. First, I brought my mother along. (Wouldn't any mom be happy her son was in the Roller Derby? NOOOOOOO!) Second, on the way there with my mom riding shotgun, I got my first speeding ticket. As I blew through a red light, I saw the flashing lights behind me and pulled over. When the officer asked me where I was going and I said to see the Roller Derby, I think it sealed my fate as he whipped out his ticket book and wrote me the citation.

When we arrived at the Coliseum there was a weird feel to the game I had never noticed before.

The New York Chiefs that night had almost lily white team of skaters and their opponent who might have been the Jersey Devils (?) just so happened to be all black. I also noticed the crowd was also divided equally. That seemed very strange to me as the teams had always been integrated and, unlike professional wrestling, race was never used in a story line, at least during my years of watching and participating. I wasn't asked to dress or skate and actually felt uncomfortable sitting there watching this black versus white match.

If my timeline is right, two nights later, this being December 6, 1973, the NY Chiefs skated in Madison Square Garden in New York City to a sold out crowd and after the game, Roller Derby owner Jerry Seltzer announced to the players and then to the world that the Roller Derby was done, over, out of business. The reason cited was the high cost of gasoline and transportation costs. Had he held on a little longer, the advent of satellite TV and "superstations" might have saved and even prospered the Roller Derby as it did professional wrestling, but alas we shall never know. A few attempts of watered down or "updated" attempts at the Derby, things like Roller Games and Roller Wars have come and gone since, but none ever came close to the popularity of the original Roller Derby. And sadly I came close, but never got to don the uniform of the New York Chiefs, but happily did get to skate the banked track in the training school.

I retired my skates thinking I'd never need eight wheels underneath me again, but as usual, I was wrong. In the fall of 1979, I had graduated college, spent four years working up to five concerts/shows a week and coming off a summer with the Grateful Dead tour, burned out on rock and roll from the operational end. So I headed back to Fort Lauderdale not sure of what my next profession would be. I was still getting calls to do concerts and was picking up shows on a per diem basis, but decided to look for a "real job."

In October of 1979 not only was disco music at its height, but so was a fad called roller disco, which consisted of young adults dancing on roller skates to the beat of disco music. This, by the way, was before the introduction of inline skates. I became a manager for Super Skating Centers of America which was a company that owned a chain of roller rinks that served as family skating rinks during the day and wild roller discos at night. Although at the time they had five rinks, I was assured because of the popularity of roller disco that the company would soon be the "McDonalds of roller skating" with a rink in every town. Although that never happened, maybe for the better, my time as the manager of the Fort Lauderdale Super Skating Center certainly was a memorable time.

While the Fort Lauderdale center was being built I helped manage the other Super Skating centers all located in the Miami area. I cemented my job with the owners on a weekday morning when they unexpectedly showed up at the center I was working in that day while we had over 300 disadvantaged black children between the ages of six and ten at the center.

The owners expected chaos, but walked into a completely different sight. At the time, the first recognized hit rap song was out called "Rappers Delight." "With a hip, hop, hip to the hippity hip hop you don't stop..." I could tell it was something new and had a good skating beat, so I had memorized the words. As the owners walked in, I was on skating floor with a portable microphone singing the song and then letting each kid sing a part. We probably played the song ten times in a row, but I looked like the Pied Piper and the kids were having the time of their lives, singing and dancing whether they could skate or not. From that moment on the owners decided I could do no wrong, which was a great position to be in as I stayed with them for the next year and a half or so.

Fort Lauderdale was a party town back in 1980 with lots of clubs and bars and none were hotter than the Fort Lauderdale Super Skating Center. Wealthy young people between eighteen and thirty (the drinking age was eighteen back then) would wait in long lines in hopes of getting in to our rink. Why? Because five nights a week between 8 p.m. and midnight for seven dollars a person, you could roller disco to your heart's content while eating from a free salad bar and having all the beer and wine you could drink. The rink had a capacity of 488 people and each night over 800 people would line up outside for a chance to get in. Taking a page from Studio 54 in New York, as manager, I would go out and scan the line prior to opening and "pick" some of the people who would be allowed in. This made me a local celebrity at bars and restaurants in the area as all the staffs and managers wanted to get in to the rink. I rarely paid for a meal or drink anywhere I went in return for letting a few folks have guaranteed entrance to the rink! They still had to pay, by the way.

This power and the popularity of our club led to one of my most embarrassing moments. I had been approached by the vice president of a popular chain of eateries at the time called Beefsteak Charlie's, his name was Kevin Ellman and he and I had an understanding. He could skate whenever he wanted without waiting in line and I could go to his restaurants and eat free whenever I wanted. These restaurants featured an endless salad bar, all the shrimp you could eat and, most importantly in my misspent youth, all the beer you cared to drink. That agreement worked out wonderfully for a long time.

A year or two after leaving Super Skating Centers, I happened to be dining with my dear friend Justin Barrett in a Beefsteak Charlie's in North Miami. Trying to relive our college days we started drinking the free beer as if we had just arrived from a month in the desert. With piles of shrimp in front of us and our main course not even ordered yet, our waitress announced we had reached the limit of how much beer she was allowed to serve to two people.

Never having heard of this before I became, with a couple of pitchers of beer imbibed, a bit indignant. "I can't believe this!" I said a bit too loud. "This is all the beer you can drink!" I continued. Looking at our poor waitress I said, "Do you know Kevin Ellman, the Vice President of this company and my personal friend?" I asked. (Keep in mind I hadn't seen nor heard of Mr. Ellman in at least two years.) I continued "If he ever heard about this, he'd tell you."

Suddenly, two tables over, I heard a voice say, "What should I tell her?" It was Kevin Ellman. I sunk deep into my seat, completely embarrassed. I finally got up and apologized to both him and our server. He luckily laughed it off, told her to keep pouring the beer and even picked up our check. Thanks, Kevin, wherever you are!

ONE PAGE WONDER

The day I turned 16 I began working at the Bath & Tennis Club Resort in Westhampton Beach, New York. I learned something that day that I never forgot as I worked with famous people through the years. Many stars stayed at the Club and there was an old Polish lady who was the maid for the suites where they stayed. I remarked to her how lucky she was to get to meet all these famous people and she said something to me that has stayed with me to this day. As I told her how lucky she was, how exciting it must be, etc., she looked at me and said "It means nothing to me; they are all slobs in the bathroom." Since that day I think I was popular with the famous simply because I didn't (in most cases) treat them any different than anyone else because in the end, *everyone* is a slob in the bathroom, so to speak.

CHAPTER 21
FLAVOR FLAV

When Shaquille O'Neal was leading the Orlando Magic to their first NBA finals in 1994, I decided I should be at their first playoff game. I had purchased one ticket way up in the rafters but arriving early at the Orena (the Orlando arena) went up to the ticket office and asked if they had any good tickets left. The attendant asked me how many tickets I needed and I said one. She said she had one in the first row courtside which I immediately bought. I then sold my original ticket at well over its face value, making up the price difference between the two tickets to this sold out event.

Excited about my good luck I went down to my courtside seat. I noticed as the game started that the 3 seats next to me were unoccupied. I wondered who would buy these great, expensive tickets and then not use them.

At the beginning of the second quarter, three black men came and sat in those seats. Seated next to me was a slight black gentleman in bib blue jeans that had been airbrushed with names and designs and he wore a giant clock around his neck. He acknowledged me as he sat down and began talking to me, but between my being hard of hearing and not fluent in Ebonics, I only understood about one tenth of what he said to me, but he kept on talking.

When he got up to go to the restroom or food stands, I noticed he climbed the bleachers rather than going to the more closely located ones. It was at this time I realized he must be someone famous as the crowd cheered him each time he climbed up the aisle and were flashing cameras and asking for autographs.

When he came back to sit down I saw written on his jeans, Flavor Flav and Public Enemy, his name and the name of his rap group and I then realized who he was. I introduced myself to him and told him some of the entertainers I had worked for.

At the end of the first half, on his way to the locker room Shaq stopped to talk to him for a moment and not only did he introduce his two friends but also introduced me, which I thought was very cool of him.

As I said earlier I had a lot of trouble keeping up with his running conversation with me. Flavor went up the bleachers to cheers and photos and returned to his seat next to me with three hot dogs.

He looked over at me and said "Frank, labrea?" I said, "Excuse me?" and he repeated, "Labrea?"

"Labrea?" I repeated, looking at him quizzically. I watched as he took each hot dog out of its roll and realized he had been asking me if I liked bread, and he was offering his hot dog rolls to me because, as he explained, he didn't like bread. I turned him down thanking him as he ate each hot dog with his fingers leaving the "brea" to be tossed away. He was a great guy and we had fun at the game, at least the part of conversation I understood. As Flavor would say, "Yeaaaaa boyeeeeee!"

ONE PAGE WONDER

Many people know the phrase "The show must go on." Some people even correctly identify it as being from the circus, but that is only really half of the phrase. On January 30, 1962 while with the Ringling Circus, the Flying Wallendas' famous seven-person pyramid on the high wire collapsed, sending two family members to their death and leaving a third a paraplegic. When Ringling officials contacted family patriarch Karl Wallenda to tell him that they need not perform again until when or if he wanted, he matter-of-factly told them the Flying Wallendas would perform in that night's show saying, "The dead are gone. The show must go on."

CHAPTER 22
JOIN THE CIRCUS

As I mentioned in the introduction, some of my first memories are of the circus and I have loved it ever since. I can remember taking the train into New York City and the old Madison Square Garden probably in 1960 or thereabouts. What I remember was seeing these old guys in torn up satin boxing robes over their street clothes talking to themselves and sparring in the air. I remember asking my mother who they were and why they acted that way and was told they were "punch drunk."

I also remember the set up of the Ringling Bros. Barnum & Bailey Circus in those days. On the "under floor" of the main arena was a large rectangular room that had a very low ceiling height and no windows, that looked as if it was used for storage when the circus wasn't in town. As you walked into this room you were slapped by the smell of the circus, an aroma made up of the mix of human and animal in this stale room. Housed in this room, along one wall were all the human sideshow performers and on the other side the menagerie of all the circus' animals with the walkway for the "marks" (patrons) in between. The sights and the smells fascinated me. I saw all the animals of the world as well as the tallest man on earth, the fattest couple, the world's smallest man, the human blockhead, the fire eater and so many more. This was the start of a fascination I still have. I have always wanted to run away with the circus.

Upstairs was the pageantry of the "big show" that has yet to be equaled for me. I go to every circus I can. I would urge you to do the same, especially if a tented circus comes your way. There are so few of those left and fewer every year. Go to a circus and appreciate these performers who literally put their lives on the line every time they perform usually six to seven days a week and two or three shows a day. The tented circus is a vanishing piece of Americana; catch it while you can.

Some of my fondest memories are of sitting in an open field on an old wooden box listening to Hoxie Tucker tell stories of his years in the circus touring with his Hoxie Bros. Circus and Great American Circus. He was an incredible man, full of stories and truly in love with the circus. When his daughter married one of the richest men in America, they begged him to come off the road or set up a permanent circus in Orlando where they were to live. But Hoxie would hear nothing of it and toured his little show for years thereafter. One of the wildest stories, and at least partially true, was about Hoxie's lion act. Hoxie owned the act and just taught the trainers what to do. The cats were well schooled in what they were to do.

One year as the start of the season approached, the "trainer" lost his nerve, couldn't get in the cage and left the show. Hoxie had no one to turn to and no way to keep these aged lions on the show without an act. So Hoxie, in old school circus tradition, thought it best to put himself and the cats out of their misery and went in the cage and shot them to death. There was a huge furor over this afterwards, as to the uninformed it might seem heartless and cruel. But it really was in all's best interest. Hoxie knew he couldn't afford to keep the meat-eating cats without an act. Lions, in captivity, breed like rabbits and there were many more lions born than ever wanted or needed so the best solution to Hoxie was just what he had done. Eventually even the courts agreed with him.

Elsewhere in this book is wire-walker Karl Wallenda's famous line, uttered after members of his family fell to their death in the matinee show, "The show must go on." Perhaps because I have been to so many circus performances I have witnessed more accidents than most. At the old Madison Square Garden, as a child I saw a lady gymnast fall to her death from the Russian sway pole. In the 1990s, I witnessed a young gymnast go from a triple somersault on a trampoline to crumpling onto the cement floor at the Orlando Arena.

There was a tiger act I never liked called Harry Thomas and His Comedy Tigers. I used to catch the act at the Long Island Game Farm in New York. I was always uneasy watching the act for a number of reasons. First, I did not like the presentation, trying to make the animals and their trainer look "funny" rather than majestic and dangerous as tigers are. Secondly, every time the trainer was in the small cage with his back to some of the tigers, his assistant was always yelling directions to him as to what tigers were not obeying or which ones to watch out for.

On one such occasion as Mr. Thomas walked by an unruly tiger it slashed at his arm. A few moments later his safari jacket arm was crimson with blood. He, in proper tradition, finished the act and hurried off. I always thought the surly behavior of his cats was partially due to the demeaning way in which the act was presented. Tigers are neither funny nor cute but majestic dangerous animals that should be presented and honored that way.

Although not the most serious injury I ever witnessed, but certainly the scariest was the one I saw at the pseudo-circus Cirque De Soleil at Disney World in Orlando, Florida. As the trapeze act was going on, two fliers collided head to head in mid-air. They both landed unconscious in the safety net about 10 feet above the stage floor. As they lay there, their bodies twitching in involuntary convulsions, no one, staff included, was sure what to do. Never having had an accident there before, the staff soon realized there was no way to lower the net to get to the bodies. Minutes went by as both bodies lay twitching in the net in full view of the sold out crowd. Then someone brought a ladder out and got into the net and shortly thereafter emergency equipment was brought in to stabilize the two still unconscious fliers. Getting them then out of the net was an even bigger chore as the net was not made to be lowered to the floor. Eventually they were removed from the net and were taken off. Again in true circus tradition, the show continued and at the end of the show, again in true circus form, an announcement was made that both performers were fine. I doubt that was truly the case but again, in circus tradition, everyone was announced as being okay.

After attending the terrible 2006 Blue unit show of the Ringling Bros. Barnum & Bailey show, sadly no longer a circus but just another touring arena show, I vowed never to spend another dollar attending a Ringling show. Gone were the tigers. Gone were the famous circus stars. Gone were the trapeze acts, human cannonball, chimps and just about everything else that makes the circus the circus. And most incredibly and sadly gone were the traditional three rings that made Ringling what it was. But up until 2006, every performer, myself included, longed to be center ring in the "big show," the Ringling Bros. Barnum & Bailey Circus.

The 2007 Ringling show titled "Bellobration" starred my friend Bello Nock and was much more a traditional show and I watched it knowing the traditional circus sadly was fading away.

To that end, it was 1983 when I applied to go to Clown College with the Ringling organization. Don Arthur was the Dean at that time and all looked good for me attending the school and then joining the Big Show. I then came up with what I thought was a brilliant idea. Since my wife Barbara was a certified and working elementary school teacher and each Ringling show carried two teachers at the time, I would volunteer her to teach on whichever show I was assigned to after graduation. When Don called me to go over some things about the school, I asked him how my wife could apply to be a teacher on the show. Finding out I was married, he informed me that the school did not allow married men in the program and, two weeks before I started, I was let go, dashing my dreams to work with Ringling. It did not end my dream of ending up in Ringling's center ring however.

While I was backstage manager at the Orange County Convention Center, I found out the circus was coming to our building and better yet not only was it Ringling Brothers but it was the unit with Gunther Gebel-Williams, Lou Jacobs, Dolly Jacobs and so many more of my favorite performers. I was in my element, renewing friendships and making new ones with Gunther, the greatest animal trainer and circus star of all time, and sitting in complete awe, talking to and listening to the then elderly Lou Jacobs, greatest of the circus clowns and his beautiful and super talented daughter Dolly Jacobs.

It was these friendships that during the circus' stay in Orlando stopped a near riot and also helped me realize my dream of being center ring with the Big Show. There were no large dressing rooms at the Center so a room had been built backstage with post and drape for the show girls to do their costume changes in. Although it had walls, it had no top. The girls noticed during one of the shows that a couple of the male spotlight operators were taking a little too long walking the catwalk to their posts, glaring down at the sometimes half dressed women. Circus people are a tight knit family and an offence to one is an offence to all. Suddenly there was a gang of men led by Gunther, whose both current and ex-wife and daughter were in the show as well, some with pipes and sticks in hand, demanding I produce the men from the catwalk. I knew that had I done that, they would have been beaten to within an inch of their life or worse. The male performers were demanding access to the catwalk or the men placed in front of them. I took Gunther and a few others I knew aside and we spoke for maybe 15 minutes and cooler heads began to prevail. I made sure the spotlight operators, if they valued their lives, stayed at their positions and never strayed for the rest of the show's stay.

I had also befriended the clowns on the show, helping them with anything they needed during the run. So when they approached me about being in their act one night, I was all for it. Since I wore a suit and had a walkie-talkie and such I looked the part I played as a security supervisor. The clowns had a pie throwing bit that ended up in a center ring climax of a clown police officer getting a pie in his face. Their idea was to replace that clown with me. We went over what was supposed to happen a few times and then suddenly I heard "Follow me!"

There I was chasing clowns around the three rings of the Greatest Show on Earth. Everything went according to plan and as I hit the spotlight of the center ring, got clobbered right in the face with a cream pie. I heard the crowd laughing and just as I thought, "Here I am, my dream came true," my foot hit some of the cream and I went straight out in the air and plopped flat on my back in center ring. The crowd roared thinking it was part of the act as the clowns helped me up and we raced off. They were laughing as hard as the crowd and saying I was a natural. I had tears in my eyes. Management at the Center wasn't very happy with me, but I really didn't care as I had fulfilled a lifelong dream and it was all and more of what I had hoped it would be.

I am proud and lucky to have circus friends. I will probably fail to mention some and I apologize ahead of time for that. But I look up to, respect and thank all my circus friends for the years of friendships and memories.

Ward Hall is the king of the sideshow. Once a staple on all circuses, Ward continues the tradition presenting a "real" circus sideshow at fairs and festivals throughout the United States. On any given day you may see the fire-eating dwarf Poobah, Spiderella the Spider Girl, a Chinese giantess, a sword swallower and the world's smallest lady, among other Wonders of the World all within the walls of his sideshow tent. I want to thank Ward for keeping the tradition alive and always treating myself and my family as true friends whenever we meet.

Tomi Leibel was a great Ringling Bros. Circus clown who set out on his own with the Leibel Family Circus. Tomi can trace his family's circus background to the early 1600s. Tomi is known for a fiery temper outside the show and as a warm, funny clown inside. I can say to me he has always been a good friend and gentleman. When my daughters, Shannon and Diana, were little, anytime we were at a performance they were treated like princesses. They basically had run of the house, riding the ponies, the elephant, playing with the other animals backstage and helping themselves to popcorn and cotton candy. When Tomi came into the ring with his coloring book pitch or balloon pitch, he always made sure the girls had a few of each and was always reluctant to take any money for them.

I would be remiss not to mention the Clyde Beatty-Cole Brothers Circus, the largest tented circus on Earth. My early recollections of the show are of Otto, the blood sweating hippopotamus, Clyde Beatty himself with his fighting lion act, and the greatest elephant presentations ever. Another staple of the show was, and I believe still is, the human cannonball act. Other shows have presented human cannonball acts, but none as well done as CBCB did. Jimmy James was the long time ringmaster and I would always look forward to seeking him out for a circus story any time the show was in town. He is a true gentleman. Sadly today, the show is known only as the Cole Brothers Circus and, for awhile, had no elephants, although recent reports have three elephants with the show. A far cry from the days when scores of elephants would run into the tent full speed, just feet from your face, you would literally feel the ground shake and feel the breeze generated by them running by. Then they would do the incredible front mount trick with each elephant standing with its front feet on the back of the pachyderm in front of him. It was an incredible sight that will never be forgotten by those who witnessed it.

Gunther Gebel-Williams was simply a superstar. He was the greatest animal trainer of all times and had that special star quality like Elvis Presley that when he walked into a space or for that matter an arena, you immediately sensed his presence and he took over the room. He was known as a taskmaster and wasn't very popular among the other circus performers. I saw a different side of Gunther though when he was out doing personal appearances and signing his autobiography. My daughter Shannon who was just turning two was with me as we went to see Gunther and get him to autograph a book for us. Prior to going I had shown Shannon pictures of Gunther and then of Gunther with some other pictures, so when I would say "Where is Gunther?" she would point to his picture each time.

As we approached Gunther at the signing, with his wife Sigrid by his side, I said to Shannon, "Where is Gunther?" and, of course, she pointed right at him. He saw this and immediately took little Shannon in his arms. With scores of people waiting, Gunther spoke to us at length, told me not to let Shannon be in the circus because it was too hard and just relished her attention. It got to the point I was feeling kind of uneasy as so many waited in line to meet Gunther, but he was in no hurry to let us go. When I suggested we go, both Gunther and Sigrid were adamant we stay. So as

Gunther signed autographs with Shannon in his lap or if the guest wanted a picture with Gunther, Shannon in Sigrid's arms, we stayed for about an hour or so. It was such a thrill for me to spend this time with this legend and the kindness and general interest he showed in us, I will never forget. Gunther Gebel-Williams, "The Lord of The Rings," passed away shortly after this on July 20, 2001. He was certainly one of a kind.

During the writing of this book another circus legend and friend of mine passed away, the great circus performer and owner Tommy Hanneford. Tommy's family members have been circus people since 1778. Along with his wife Struppi, a great aerialist and tiger trainer in her own right, he treated my daughters like his own wherever and whenever we met him. As a young boy growing up in the circus, he became one of the best horseback riders of all time following in his uncle "Poodles" Hanneford's footsteps. But one of the first acts he performed in the circus was the rolla bolla. You may have seen this act in a circus where a board is placed on top of a cylinder and a person balances on it. Both of my daughters Shannon and Diana can rolla bolla and they told Tommy this once when we met him at a circus convention. He told them all about his rolla bolla act and from then on whenever we ran into the Hannefords, Tommy would say, "There are my rolly bolly girls!"

If we were at a performance of the Royal Hanneford Circus, at a convention, or just had a chance meeting on the street, we were always treated like family with Tommy and Struppi Hanneford. One thing I always remember was whenever we were saying goodbye, Struppi would always say, "Never say goodbye, just say 'until next time!'" Sadly we did have to say goodbye to Tommy Hanneford who passed away on December 5, 2005. He is gone but not forgotten and the Royal Hanneford Circus continues making history under the direction of his incredible wife and our friend Struppi Hanneford.

The legendary circus owner, human blowtorch, sword swallower and sideshow owner John Strong is a new friend that I look forward to cutting jackpots (sharing circus stories) with for years to come.

As I stated earlier, if you get a chance to go to a real circus, preferably a tented show, please do, no matter your age or state of mind. It will take you to a place that soon will only be in people's memories. Sawdust, cotton candy, elephants and tent dreams... there is *nothing* better.

Author, Miss Dolly, & Lou Jacobs

Lou Jacobs & Author

CHAPTER 23
SINGER LUTHER VANDROSS

I was lucky enough to work a series of "Soulfests" put on originally by Budweiser beer. These were great stadium shows with superstar lineups. One of these shows featured The O'Jays and Luther Vandross among many others. I was excited to see The O'Jays because one of their members Sammy Strain was from my hometown Westhampton Beach. I grew up as friends with his brother Tommy and knew his younger sister Paulette as well. Sammy was with Little Anthony and the Imperials for years before joining The O'Jays and is now performing with Little Anthony again. It was great meeting him and he and the other O'Jays who had been out to Westhampton had a great time reminiscing with me.

But the highlight of the evening was Luther Vandross' appearance. He had an incredible voice and put on a great show. The funniest part of the show to me was one of his encores. He came back onstage to the predominantly black crowd and began the great Sam Cooke song, "We're Having a Party." The crowd was really into it, singing and swaying to the song, but all of a sudden the crowd went wild. As I looked up over the front of the stage I saw Luther's lady backup singers come out onstage and the reaction was to the way they were dressed. Three of the ladies were dressed in giant Colonel Sanders Kentucky Fried Chicken buckets and the other three were dressed in giant orange soda bottles. The crowd just went crazy. Now if I were to suggest the stereotype that all black people like fried chicken and orange soda I would be vilified for it. But when Luther suggested it, everyone thought it was the best thing ever! If you never had the chance to see Luther Vandross live, it was an exceptional event. If you have never listed to a Luther Vandross CD, do yourself a favor and listen to one of the most gifted singers ever. He was taken from us much too soon.

CHAPTER 24
100,000 ELVIS FANS CAN'T BE WRONG

Little did I know that as a thirteen-year-old in 1968 I would see an entertainer on television that would change my life. The music of the time for teenagers certainly was NOT the music of Elvis Presley, but once I saw his '68 Comeback Special I was hooked. He had that personality component that has always intrigued me. Women would scream not only at his performance, although they certainly did that too, but just at his mere presence. So at age 13, in 1968, I became a lifelong Elvis Presley fan. I could never have imagined how much he would change my life forever. So as others were listening to the exploding rock music scene, I was delving into Elvis music, particularly his live performances. I enjoyed the music of the day as well but always went back to Elvis.

Other teenagers thought I was crazy. I further cemented that idea in their heads when I appeared on our school television channel as Elvis, mimicking his every move as I lip-synched to his '68 Comeback songs. Each day for a week there was a different song and I was, if nothing else, the talk of the school for that week and forever linked with Elvis with all my high school friends. On the last day of the show, I was watching the tape as it appeared on televisions throughout our school. As I walked out of the studio into the school hallway, I was mobbed by a group of young ladies with cameras and autograph books screaming "Oh, Elvis!" and tearing my clothes off. For a moment or two I was dumbfounded, but decided to play the part, posing for pictures and signing all the autographs as requested. This idol stuff wasn't so bad after all.

The next Elvis stepping stone in my life is when I heard he would be appearing at Madison Square Garden in New York City for a series of concerts. I was seventeen at the time and determined to see that show. I was lucky enough to get tickets to the Saturday afternoon matinee show and took a date (who could have cared less) to see Elvis. He had me in complete awe. Shortly thereafter when the record (yes, record; there were no CDs back then!) came out, I memorized every word and recalled every move, playing that disc over and over and over. Today the recording of the Saturday matinee performance is available on a CD entitled *An Afternoon at the Garden* for your listening pleasure. I was there! Just when my attention to Elvis might have waned, then came 1973's "Elvis: Aloha from Hawaii," the first television special to be beamed live by satellite worldwide, attracting a record-breaking audience of over 1.5 billion viewers in more than 40 countries.

While the music world continued to change and I kept up with all of it, Elvis was still my hero. When it was announced Elvis would do two shows near my hometown in Long Island, New York, at the Nassau Coliseum, I of course got tickets to both shows. I attended the afternoon show with the incredible and eccentric entertainer Hugh Shannon, who has his own chapter in this book, then raced back home, dropped him off, picked up my date (another young lady who could have cared less about Elvis), and raced back for the evening show. I couldn't get enough.

Today, both Lisbeth Dahlen and Charlene Halsey, the two girls I had taken as dates to these Elvis concerts, realize how lucky they were to have seen The King and just how historically and musically significant these events had been. At this point, I had seen Elvis live three times, imitated him thousands of times, and was off to college to put it all behind me. Or so I thought.

While attending Biscayne College, I was also very busy as the backstage manager of the Hollywood Sportatorium, running everything from car shows to boxing matches to concerts of all types. When I was called into the owner's office on the afternoon of February 10, 1977, I had no idea what was in store. I kept thinking what I had done wrong that might have gotten back to them. Letting friends in free to shows and special friends backstage was a common practice, but it was the only thing I could think of that they might be angry about. There were rarely any private meetings unless it was a termination. I hoped I hadn't done anything that bad as I was having the time of my life, running these shows, meeting the performers, and generally being in charge of all the show's workings from the stage front through to the backstage exit where the performers and their equipment exited. What could I have done to be fired? I was sweating bullets as I entered the office. There sat Debbie Johnson, co-owner of the Hollywood Sportatorium, with her husband, Bruce, and his father, Norman. I was beckoned to sit down and felt sure this was the end. Should I plead for my life to try and hold on to some job at the arena, just walk out, or fight off tears telling them how much I loved my job?

Debbie Johnson spoke, "Frank, we have a show coming up and we were wondering if you would rather work it or just attend it?" What kind of question was that? I had worked EVERY show at the arena and certainly wasn't interested in just being a concertgoer. "I don't understand the question," I countered. "Well if you weren't able to do your normal professional job obviously we wouldn't want you in charge backstage," Debbie retorted. What was going on? What were they talking about? My confused look led Debbie to continue, "Elvis is coming in next week and knowing how you love him, we didn't want you backstage if you were going to pass out or something when you met him." I had to play this very cool. I took a deep breath. "No, I'll work it. It's just another show to me." I tried to look very composed as I shook their hands and left the office.

Just another show?! Fireworks were going off in my head and I am sure I have never smiled wider. I was not only going to be Elvis Presley's backstage manager, but was going to be able to actually shake his hand! I was walking on clouds. I was going to meet my hero!

February 12, 1977, Elvis Presley was appearing at the Hollywood Sportatorium Arena and I was his backstage manager! As his entourage slowly trickled in backstage, I of course, knew almost everyone by name and I think that impressed most everyone as they were all very friendly towards me. The opening act of the show was comedian Jackie Kahane and I remember him being very cordial. My biggest kick early on was standing at the dressing room door of Elvis' lady backup vocal group, The Sweet Inspirations, and singing along to their songs. They eventually noticed me standing there and invited me in! I was singing with The Sweet Inspirations! I only stayed a few minutes, but was already on cloud nine.

The show started and Elvis was not yet at the arena. I was wondering how he would arrive and when. It was at this point that one of his traveling entourage came to me to discuss Mr. Presley's arrival. The plan was for his bus to pull up directly to his dressing room door and he would leave the bus and go directly into the dressing room. My job was to make sure this entire area was clear of everyone and then I was to lock the door into the arena so the area was sealed until he was in his dressing room. This meant I was not going to be able to see or meet him upon his arrival. I assured him all would work according to plan. But was he kidding? Did he really think I wasn't going to be there the first time Elvis entered my building?

Everyone was anxiously awaiting Elvis' bus when we heard there was a problem. The road leading into our arena was a two lane rural road and we were located literally in the middle of Everglades swamp. Oddly enough, that land today is in the middle of a city, so when someone says they have some Florida swampland to sell you, it might be a good deal. Anyway, about a quarter mile down the single road in and out of the arena, they spotted an old abandoned cabin that had caught fire. Elvis' people were worried if he saw the fire he would be upset about it and/or want to pay for the rebuilding of it. So they were slowing the bus down in hopes that by the time he drove past it, the fire would be less noticeable, if not out.

It seemed like an eternity, but I soon saw the bus pulling up. I cleared the area of everyone and then locked the arena entrance per instruction, but I stayed on the outside of the door. I think someone yelled, "Get inside!" but I retorted, "Can't, doors locked!" My heart was beating a mile a minute. Yes, I had met so many rock stars and celebrities, but this was The King, Elvis Presley. The bus door opened and a bevy of beautiful women were ushered off the bus and all went and stood in a corner of the deserted backstage alley area. Again it seemed like an eternity and then Elvis came walking off the bus. I walked up to him and said "Hi, Mr. Presley. Welcome to the Hollywood Sportatorium. I'm Frank Lynch, your backstage manager." He shook my hand and said, "Nice to meet you, Frank," before disappearing into his dressing room. I also remember getting a couple dirty looks from the Memphis Mafia for greeting Elvis, but as I said, even if it meant me losing my job, I was going to meet The King.

I stayed posted outside the dressing room as The Sweet Inspirations came off stage from their set and intermission began. As I stood there I thought of all the things I could have and should have done. I should have given Elvis a token gift of our appreciation of his appearance. I should have gotten a picture with him. On and on my mind raced until I saw the houselights go down and heard the call in my radio... "Showtime!"

All the backup singers were scurrying back onstage and then Joe Guercio led the orchestra in the theme song from *2001: A Space Odyssey* and then the Memphis Mafia exploded from the dressing room with Elvis in tow. I jumped right in front to get Elvis to the stage in the same way I got every other performer up there. As we raced through the door into the runway to the stage, I did not see but heard that Elvis ran face first into the corner of the door. Whether he did or not (remembering this was only six months before he died and was in poor health), once the spotlight hit him, he was off and running like nothing had happened. I positioned myself in the barricade between the stage and the audience and wherever Elvis went onstage I was there just below him in the barricade.

As he sang each and every song, so did I. I'm not sure that Elvis noticed, but most of the performers on stage did and certainly got a kick out of it. At some point I finally remembered the little Instamatic camera in my pocket and then, against every rule, took the tiny camera out to snap a picture. Elvis saw me pull out the camera and it must have amused him somewhat as he posed for the picture and gave me one of his famous smiles.

Throughout the show, which also is now available on CD (*A Hot Time in Florida*), I mirrored Elvis, being just in front and below him wherever he went onstage and, of course, singing all the while. It seemed like only moments later Elvis was singing "Can't Help Falling in Love" and it was time for him to leave the stage.

Elvis never did encores and everyone knew once "Can't Help Falling" started, it would be his last song. I've never felt the electricity in a crowd the way I did that night during his performance. As Elvis appeared, before the spotlight even hit Elvis at the beginning of the show, flashbulbs lit up the entire darkened arena as bright as day. And other than when Elvis gestured for the crowd to be quiet, the noise level was incredible, women screaming over and over "Elvis, Elvis," plus all the cheering and applauding. I stationed myself at the bottom of the stage steps and as Elvis came off he was surrounded by the Memphis Mafia security and at a full run I led them out the arena door to the bus waiting for him. He jumped in and they were off property before the music stopped.

Elvis had truly left the building. As the other show members left the stage, I spoke to most, thanking them and telling them what a great show it had been. When The Sweet Inspirations came off, they gathered around me and said, "You really DO know our music, don't you? We saw you singing, but not just singing Elvis' part, singing everyone's part!"

I explained to them I had been singing those songs every day for the last five years so it was natural to me. We hugged and they were off. The only sounds left were the crew breaking down the stage as I walked through the empty arena. It was unlike any other show I had ever done or would ever do. It seemed to pass in a matter of moments in a way that was almost surreal or dreamlike. I was exhilarated to have met Elvis and all the entourage. Little did I know at that point, Elvis was going to stay in my life forever.

I, of course, continued to be a big Elvis fan thereafter, even though I was working with The Rolling Stones, ELO, The Grateful Dead and others. It was an odd mix, but loving all types of music was no problem to me. I saw that Elvis was to again play a concert at the Nassau Coliseum on Long Island. So I called my friends from Graceland and they sent me tickets and backstage passes for the show set for August 22, 1977. They also said they might need me to work, so I was thrilled that I would meet Elvis again. My plan was to take a break from working shows in Florida and go up to New York to visit family and friends and then see the show.

August 15, 1977 started like any other summer Sunday in the Hamptons on Long Island. I attended church that morning and then made plans to meet friends that afternoon at a local watering hole called The Mad Hatter. This is the bar where many up and coming bands of the day played, bands like Twisted Sister, The Good Rats, Rat Race Choir and others. They drew a large and raucous weekend afternoon crowd for their weekend happy hours that featured a live band, free admission, 50 cent mixed drinks, free hot dogs and five beers for a dollar. (Remember, this was 1977.) The crowds were always large and rowdy and a great time was always had by all.

Having not seen many of my old high school friends for awhile, our meeting at the Hatter got a bit out of control in terms of alcohol consumption. As happy hour ended and goodbyes were said, I poured myself out to my car. I could barely walk so driving wasn't a great idea either, but my car seemed to have autopilot from the Hatter back to my house, having made that trip under such conditions too many times. Incredibly, as always, I made it home safely. I was not looking forward to facing my parents in this condition and had hoped to just stumble through the house to bed.

As I staggered in I was met face-to-face by my mother who said, "You had a call from Memphis. I have the number written down." I replied, "I need to lie down. I'll call them back later." My mom was perturbed I was drunk and said, "You may not need to; Elvis is dead." I couldn't believe what she had said. I suddenly felt even worse than I had, if that was possible. I turned on the television to verify the sad news. By this time it had been a few hours since the news broke. I started to call the airlines to try and get a flight to Memphis, but there were none. All the planes were full and all the phone lines tied up. I was in shock. The only thing I could think to do was exactly what I did do. I called a taxi and had them take me back to The Mad Hatter. I sat at the bar and further drowned my sorrows as those around me partied unaware of the day's tragedy.

After Elvis' death I thought my connection to him was gone, but as he had been in life, he was larger-than-life in death as well. It has been well documented his estate made more money after his death than he made during his life. Of course, one of the reasons for that was there was money flowing in but no one to spend it, especially the way Elvis did, giving away cars, jewelry and such on the spur of the moment.

When Six Flags decided to close their Orlando attraction, I was going to be out of a job. There was an Elvis Presley museum down the strip from Six Flags and I applied there and with my Presley provenance, was hired as one of the two managers. I really didn't know much about the museum nor its owner, Jimmy Velvet, at the time. The museum itself had quite a few nice exhibits including Elvis' last car, the race car from the movie Spinout, as well as his birth records and even some of his credit cards and lots more.

I was amazed at the number of people who came through the museum each day and met lots of characters. Everyone who came through the door seemed to have an Elvis story or connection. It amazed me. One gentleman came in, who I guessed to be in his mid-20s, and on one side of his face he was clean-shaven, but on the other he had a long Elvis-style mutton chop sideburn. After staring at him I just had to ask what his story was. He said ever since Elvis' death he wore the one sideburn in tribute to his fallen idol. My thought was to ask him why he didn't wear two to balance out his head, but I didn't want to set him off. On many occasions people came out of the museum crying. I was never quite sure why looking at a car or a credit card could drive someone to tears, but again it was the magic that was Elvis. I have never learned to be untrusting.

When I first met the museum owners, Jimmy and Kathy Velvet, I thought they were great people and believed all the stories that Jimmy spun. He told me he was a famous recording artist and a close friend of Elvis' and that Elvis and Elvis' father, Vernon, gave him most of his collection, which was large enough that at one time I think he had five or six museums open throughout the country. I then started to learn the true facts, which were always a bit different than the way Jimmy had told them to me.

I learned that when Elvis was alive, Jimmy had set up a store/museum directly across the street from Elvis' home in Graceland. Rather than Elvis providing the items for the museum, anyone who had access to Graceland knew if they left Graceland with any item, be it a lamp, spoon, or piece of discarded carpet, they could take it to Jimmy across the street and he would buy it. Through the years, he acquired more and more items and became, according to Elvis estate sources, more and more irritating, until after Elvis' death when the estate bought the property he had his museum on and moved him out.

A classic example of Jimmy's "showmanship", for lack of a better word, was a pair of Elvis' solid gold TCB eyeglasses that were on display in the museum. Along with the glasses was a letter from the lady to whom Elvis had given the glasses. It was addressed to Jimmy and stated although she treasured the glasses and hated to sell them they were for sale for $100,000, so she could pay for her son's upcoming college education. With the letter and glasses in the display you would be led to believe Jimmy must have paid that amount to her since he now had the glasses. When I questioned him about it I said, "Jimmy you paid $100,000 for those glasses?" and he assured me that he had. I later learned he traded a Camaro automobile for the glasses and shortly thereafter the woman's son was killed in it when he crashed it at a high speed.

Most of my time at the museum was fun and it gave me the idea to open my own museum, "Frank Lynch's Rock & Roll Museum," with all the memorabilia I had collected over the years. I also bought and sold a lot of memorabilia during this time, and of course looking back, wish I had kept it all. I bought a great complete set of Elvis' records from when he was on the Sun label, consisting of five 45s and five 78s. After purchasing them I was contacted by the president of the Denmark Elvis Presley Fan Club who offered me three times the amount I had paid for the set. He was also willing to fly over to pay and pick them up. Today I regret selling them, but at the time the profit seemed worth it. Not only did he fly over to Orlando to pick them up, he also interviewed me and a few months later I received a Danish magazine with a three-page article on me and this gentleman's quest to America for the treasured Sun records.

My Elvis connection continued on and on, even in the most unexpected places. In Las Vegas, I was wearing my Elvis tour jacket and kept getting stopped for pictures and autographs even though I assured the folks I was no one who's autograph they needed.

In 1980, when I was the backstage manager of the Orange County Civic Center in Orlando, we held the huge International Association of Travel Agents trade show. One of the booths was from Graceland. They were just opening Graceland as an attraction and I started talking to the Graceland representatives about my Elvis experiences. It seems almost comical now that at the time they really were not sure whether Graceland would be viable as a tourist destination when, of course, now it is so successful.

Among the people I met that convention was Mr. Jack Soden, the president of Elvis Presley Enterprises, responsible for overseeing everything Elvis, from Graceland to souvenirs bearing The King's image. We had some long talks about Elvis and the hoped for success of Graceland. He told me if I ever got up to Graceland to be sure and look him up. I never forgot that invite and 22 years later decided I needed to make the pilgrimage to Graceland and take my children to experience Elvis. I called Jack and reminded him of his promise from long ago. He actually remembered me and told me to be sure and look him up when we got to Graceland.

Of course, we stayed at the Heartbreak Hotel, street address? "Down at the end of Lonely Street." We took the tour through Graceland and Elvis' planes, etc., and afterwards we all got to go up to the executive office and have a great chat with Jack Soden. He was so cordial and treated us like family. He still is in charge out there and I wish him all the best. We have even exchanged a few emails about me becoming involved with Elvis Presley Enterprises in some regard, so the Elvis connection may never end.

Elvis in Miami February 12, 1977

Elvis & Richard Nixon

CHAPTER 25
THE ROCK & ROLL MUSEUM

While working at the Elvis museum people kept telling me, "Frank, you have more stuff than this and it's from lots of famous people. Why don't you open a museum attraction?" Finally I decided to try it. I rented a storefront on International Drive in Orlando, the tourist strip, and transformed it into a museum and gift shop. It was a labor of love, but in the two years we were there we broke even and then decided to close. I found out you had to sell a LOT of concert tee shirts to offset the high rent in that area.

Among the people I got to know during this time were the guys from Mötley Crüe when they were the hottest band around. They liked coming to Orlando when they had a few days off from touring and also loved playing in the Central Florida area. Tommy Lee, their drummer, and sometimes the other guys would stop by the museum when dining at their favorite restaurant, The Crab Shack, which was located just behind my museum. Not only were they great guys, but whenever they dropped by, sales at the museum soared. Crüe fans came to see us not only because of the band dropping by, but also because we had a large Mötley Crüe exhibit, including one of Nikki Sixx's complete stage outfits.

They seemed like really nice guys to me, but their antics in Orlando were legendary. They were thrown out of Walt Disney World because someone in their suite at the Polynesian Hotel tossed a chair off the balcony and hit an innocent passerby below. They were also infamous for renting out some of Orlando's elaborate go-kart tracks, demolishing all the karts and just writing a check for the damage.

When I spoke to Bryn Bridenthal, their publicist, about all the crazy stories she told me "Not only are they true, but you only hear 1/100th of what they do. That's why they have me as a publicist, to hide the rest of the hijinks." I could only imagine. At the end of this chapter is a picture of my wife Barbara holding the Rock & Roll Museum logo while posing with Mötley Crüe backstage in Orlando. I am standing next to Nikki Sixx in the picture... well, would have been had the ace photographer I had brought along gotten the shot right. Instead, as you'll see, I was cut out of the picture. Needless to say we never used that photographer again.

We had many exhibits in the museum, including platinum and gold award albums, stage costumes, personal belongings and such, many of which had been given to me during my days with the bands. I had Molly Hatchet's "Flirtin With Disaster" confederate flag guitar, ZZ Top's hats, and a large "brick" from *The Wall* that the members of Pink Floyd had signed and lots more.

At the time I didn't have many Beatles pieces, so I wrote Yoko Ono and asked for her help. A week or so later the phone rang and it was Yoko Ono calling! She said she was interested in giving me something from John Lennon, but wanted to verify that there really was an attraction. She was very nice and of course I was shocked to even be talking to her. A few days later, I received a package with an autographed photo of Yoko and a gold sales album award that was presented to John Lennon for one of the Beatles albums. When we closed the museum most of the pieces were sent to California and auctioned off but the things Yoko sent me are still in my possession.

It was during my time at the museum that on a frigid February morning I walked outside the front entrance to watch the skies for the launch of the space shuttle Challenger. I remember thinking with the temperature so low they would probably scrub the launch, but a few moments later I saw the craft blast off. As I watched it go up I will never forget seeing it break into 3 distinct pieces and the trident of smoke from each piece formed in the sky. I knew something had gone terribly wrong and went back into the museum and turned on the radio to hear of the tragedy of the Challenger.

That being my saddest memory, my happiest was a lady who rushed into the museum gift shop one morning to buy two of our museum tee shirts for her son. These shirts had been designed by my lifelong friend and great unappreciated artist, Chris Kavan. The lady said she had to tell me that with Disney, Universal, Sea World and all the rest, her teenage son's favorite attraction was our museum so she wanted to surprise him with the shirts. It was a great thing to hear that we were actually appreciated among the theme park giants.

Mötley Crüe with Barbara Lynch

Author & Jake E. Lee from Ozzy's Band

Author & Twisted Sister's AJ Pero

Twisted Sister's Dee Snider

CHAPTER 26
THANK YOU, JIMMY BUFFET

Another performer who has seemed to stay in my life is the Key West troubadour Jimmy Buffet. Back in the mid 1970s while working shows in Miami, I witnessed the start of his rise to superstardom. From playing Miami theaters that held less than 1500 people to the constant sellouts of major arenas, Jimmy did well for himself preaching a lifestyle to which most of us living in Miami at that time subscribed. In the early days, Jimmy's traveling group was really like a family, performers and roadies, people like "Fingers" Taylor on harmonica, James Utley on keyboard, and Hobbit running things for Jimmy backstage. Hobbit later ran Jimmy's incredible tee shirt company. This all of course was before there was a corporate Jimmy Buffet with restaurants, clothing lines and fans known as "parrot heads."

I am always being asked "Are you a parrot head?" and I always answer, "No, I was a Jimmy Buffet fan and friend BEFORE there were parrot heads," and that is the case. I was working Jimmy's Florida shows as early as 1975. Any show he had that I didn't work, I went to, supporting the ideal of the tropical laidback Caribbean lifestyle. I remember while vacationing in the Hamptons in the summer of 1976, I heard Jimmy was playing at Belmont Racetrack on Long Island after the races. I talked my friend Chris Kavan into going with me for a day of gambling on the horses and some Jimmy music to top it off. The Jimmy crew was shocked to see me standing there in front of the stage in New York and not in Florida. I was shocked that only a couple hundred people (if that) stayed for the show. Jimmy was great as always.

As I stated, I watched Jimmy's popularity and empire grow through the years. I still maintain I need at least one Jimmy concert a year to rejuvenate me and refresh my Caribbean soul. Back in the early 1990s, many of Jimmy's original gang were gone and the days of just showing up at concerts and being let in were on the wane. After getting some free tickets to attend a Jimmy show in Orlando, I took a couple of old backstage passes along, just in case backstage security wasn't as good as I had once been. My wife Barbara took along Jimmy's children's book, *Jolly Mon*, in hopes of having him sign it for our then-young daughter Shannon. Jimmy never disappoints show-wise and I waved to a few remaining old friends as I saw them come on and off stage.

After the show we donned our 15-year-old backstage passes, I flashed them to the guard and walked backstage. I thought to myself, "My guys never would have fallen for that." Backstage, we talked to Michael Utley for a few minutes and Barbara had the book out in her hands. An unknown staff member came up and out of the blue said, "Are you waiting for Jimmy to sign that?" She nodded and we were whisked into a small room where we were standing alone with Jimmy sitting on a couch relaxing. We were both so shocked we weren't sure what to do. Barbara asked if he'd sign the book "To Shannon," which he did and we said thanks, told him it had been a great show as always, and left. I know he didn't recognize me from years before and we didn't think to ask to get our picture with him or even go into our past meetings.

I'll probably never get another chance to be alone with or have a serious conversation with Jimmy, but who knows, he may read this. So Jimmy: thanks for all the fun, all the great music (I tear up every time I hear my anthem, "A Pirate Looks at Forty," it tells the story of my life), all the paychecks, all the tee shirts, and for reminding us all that we shouldn't ever take life too seriously. I owe you a cheeseburger in *my* paradise, the island of Eleuthera in the Bahamas, the next time we are both over there.

In college, my roommate Rick Berry loved to take his golf clubs and go out into the hallway of our dorm and smash golf balls down the long hallway, watching them ping off the walls and floor like a super ball. Of course, this could be very dangerous to anyone who opened their dorm room door and stepped out into the hallway during this barrage. One morning, Rick asked me to go watch him hit a few balls down the hall.

He had hit a few with the expected amusing results when he really got into one. The ball screamed off the club head like a line drive in baseball. It was a straight shot about five feet high and on a line towards the far end of the dorm. A few milliseconds before it hit the doors at the far end of the hallway, one of the priests, Father Martin, opened the door to walk in.

As he stepped in, the ball shot up over his head, exploding the exit sign over his head. Realizing he had just escaped possible death, Father Martin yelled, "Rick, what do you think you are doing?!" Without missing a beat, Rick said, "Practicing my seven-iron, Father!" and took his clubs back in our room and closed the door.

CHAPTER 27
THE MANY FACES OF MICHAEL JACKSON

Michael Jackson was, at the very least, a strange and incredible talent. But what people sometimes fail to remember is during the early 1980s he was the biggest superstar ever. And if you had the chance to see him perform live, there is no doubt he was one of the greatest entertainers ever. I have waited until near the end of writing of this book to pen this chapter because it seemed that, up until his untimely death and since, there is a bizarre Michael Jackson story every few minutes and I was waiting to see if any of those would ever be resolved.

But before we go into the bizarre, let's go back to my first contact with Michael and how we ended up becoming friends. In 1983, Michael Jackson was the King of Pop. He was a trend setter and literally making over a million dollars a day in royalties. As with most of the other celebrities, little did I know he was going to just walk into my life.

Around that time, I was the manager of Six Flags Stars Hall of Fame in Orlando. One day while I was in the box office talking to our ticket sellers, I noticed a scruffy-looking man walking toward the ticket window. He reminded me a bit of the comedian Redd Foxx. He asked to speak to the manager and I walked outside and met him on the sidewalk. He asked me what we did for celebrities who came through our museum. I thought it an odd question considering his disheveled appearance, but told him we had a security staff and that I myself had worked security and backstage duties for many stars and rock groups. At this point he said, "Follow me," and I did although I wasn't sure why. As we were walking down the long walkway from the attraction to the parking area, the only thing the man asked was my name. I started wondering what I was doing, following some stranger to the parking lot when I had all the keys to the building on me; for all I knew he could have mugged me. We got to the parking area and there was a small red rental car sitting there, running. The man opened the back door of the car and said, "Frank Lynch meet Michael Jackson. Michael, this is Frank, the manager here. He'll be showing you around." I, of course, was stunned.

I knew Michael loved Orlando and had his own suite at Disney World at the time, but never did I expect to come face-to-face with him and certainly not in this manner. As we walked up the long sidewalk, I kept thinking it must have been a joke or a Michael look-alike, but it was really him.

As we entered the museum both the staff and the public acted as I did. No one rushed up to him or asked for a picture or autograph because they were so stunned to see him they thought, "Well it can't really be him." Michael and I walked through the world's largest wax museum and we stopped at almost every exhibit. It got to be kind of a trivia game as he would ask me a question about a certain movie or star and I'd ask him one back. We probably spent two or more hours in the museum that day and then, as quickly as he appeared, he disappeared.

A few days went by and when I came into work after a day off, I was told that the disheveled older man who had taken me to Michael that first day had been back to the museum a few times asking for me. I had learned he was Michael's personal assistant and I think I remember his first name as Fred. Barely 15 minutes after my arrival at work, there was Fred asking me to walk out and escort Michael into the museum again. Fred told me as we walked out that Michael wanted to come back, but would only get out of the car if I was there. So again, as we had a few days prior, we walked through the museum and this time took in the show presented there called "The Rock and Roll Time Machine." It was a bit strange sitting with him through the presentation which had bits of Michael and the Jackson 5 all through the movie. He seemed to enjoy the show as I remember.

For about two weeks straight it seemed almost every day I worked Michael would show up and we'd go through the museum. He would always stand and stare for long periods of time at the wax figure we had of Diana Ross as Billie Holiday in *Lady Sings the Blues.* Michael would always say, "You know Frank, Diana Ross is much prettier than that in real life." The first time he said it, I reminded him this was her portraying Billie Holiday, who aside from being a huge talent was also a drug addict and not always at her most glamorous. After that initial response, I would just agree with him. Of course as his plastic surgeries started, many were led to observe he was trying to make himself look like Diana Ross. Maybe I am partially to blame for allowing him to stand there staring at her for up to half an hour at a time.

One of my most memorable moments was sitting in my office one day reading the magazine Billboard, I turned the page to a full page ad announcing "The Victory Tour," The Jackson's long awaited reunion tour. As I looked up from the paper, who was standing in the doorway, but Michael himself. I asked him if he had seen the ad. He said he had only seen the proof, so I showed it to him and asked him to autograph it, which he did. I still have that one-of-a-kind piece of memorabilia framed in my office.

Michael and I actually had a great time, eventually playing loads of trivia and discussing other things as we went along day after day through Stars Hall of Fame. On the occasion when someone did ask for an autograph, Michael would always sign but rarely did anything more than that. At times he would continue walking and practically toss the autograph over his shoulder as he walked away. At first I thought it rude but I came to see he was very shy and really didn't want any eye or verbal contact with anyone he didn't know.

One day I brought up the idea that we really needed a Michael Jackson figure in the museum and could tell he liked the idea. He invited me to his suite, The Michael Jackson Suite, at the Royal Plaza Hotel in Downtown Disney to discuss the idea further. When I arrived at his suite, his manager Frank DiLeo greeted me and said Michael would be right out. One of the staff members at the hotel also worked as a Michael Jackson look-alike and whenever Michael wanted something from the hotel, he wanted his look-alike to deliver it. Soon after I arrived the look-alike was at the door with a bottle of mineral water. Michael appeared, took the water from the look-alike, a strange scene to witness, gave him a $100 bill and disappeared back into the bedroom. I remarked to Dileo, "That was a $100 tip!" He said "Frank, as we stand here right now, Michael is making over $100,000 an hour in royalties, so for him to give a $100 tip is like you giving someone a dime tip."

Michael reappeared and we had a great conversation about a possible figure for our museum, what pose it should be, the scene it would be placed in, etc. I took some pictures so our artists could do a sketch mock up for Michael's approval. He and I also discussed building a Michael Jackson museum and some of the things it might include. We discussed an awards room, a holographic Michael greeting people, a theater and a zoo, as well as a possible dark ride. Michael also wanted me to look into doing an audio-animatronic figure of him as well, either for a possible museum or for his own home, "like the ones at Disney." I left saying we'd stay in touch and I would see him with his brothers on the Victory Tour coming to Jacksonville the next month.

When I now show someone the pictures I have of Michael and me, I always say, "These are old pictures, you can tell; I had hair and Michael was black." We both have changed a lot over the years.

When my wife Barbara and I arrived in Jacksonville the night of the concert, our names were nowhere to be found on any guest list. Eventually someone came out and said to follow them and we were led to the VIP box. There we were with 70,000 people below us and the massive Victory Tour stage to our left. Even more to our amazement we were seated with Patti Labelle, Lionel Ritchie and Michael's parents! The show, Michael, the crowd and the performance were all incredible. It really did remind me of the electricity of an Elvis concert. And you could tell that Michael left everything onstage for his audience. We would later hear he left the stage each night in complete exhaustion, dehydrated and in pain and I could absolutely believe that watching him. We had taken him a gift, an airbrushed soft sculpture of Marilyn Monroe, and wanted to give it to him backstage. By the time we got back there he had gone, but I gave the gift to one of his entourage I recognized. I know he got it because a year or more later there was a television show that highlighted his home at Neverland and I saw the piece I had given him on one of the walls. Little did I know at the time I would never see him again, nor know the even more bizarre life and death he would have.

Soon thereafter, Six Flags decided to close their Orlando attraction, Stars Hall of Fame and my connection to Michael Jackson was lost. I wrote to him on a number of occasions mentioning the museum idea and finally received a short response from his manager Frank DiLeo saying they were not interested in pursuing the museum idea at that time. I know in my heart that Michael never saw any of my letters as I know he was still very interested in the museum concept and especially in his own audio-animatronic robot figure.

The problems that Michael had encountered over the years came from being too famous. You have to remember he was famous by the time he was five years old. He grew up in a cocoon and never had a chance to experience any of the things that normal people do, the things that shape their lives and make them the adult they become. Michael never got to play with other children. He never fell out of a tree. He never dated nor got stood up on a date and didn't attend school. So all the things that turned you and I into the people we are today never happened to him so he wasn't sure how to make mature decisions. Being surrounded by people who work for you your whole life is a hard and horrible existence as well. It is why I think he liked coming to talk to me, because I wasn't after anything from him and I always found him polite and intelligent. Keep in mind this was a very rich, very eccentric man child and an easy target for those looking to make easy money by besmirching his name. His never was an easy life to live. More than anything, I felt very sorry for Michael and think of him as a tragic genius.

People always ask me from when I knew him, would I have let my children stay at Neverland and the answer is I would, without hesitation. While he was eccentric, in my mind, and in his one court case, he was not guilty of any of the sensational accusations targeted at him. The closing of Neverland did not shock me nor did Michael living abroad. After all he had gone through here in the States with not only individuals but the police and court systems harassing him, could you blame him?

Michael left us unexpectedly on June 25, 2009, on the verge of a comeback tour that would have re-established him as the King of Pop and, in my mind, would have ended up in a triumphant world tour, so everyone could once again see the greatest onstage entertainer of all time. Tragically now that will never happen and I will miss you, Michael.

Michael Jackson & Author at Stars Hall of Fame
Previously Unpublished Photo

At Michael Jackson's funeral:
"There was nothing strange about your daddy.
It was strange what your daddy had to deal with."
- Rev. Al Sharpton

Michael Jackson & Author
Previously Unpublished Photo

Michael Jackson
Previously Unpublished Photo

CHAPTER 28
THE SQUARED CIRCLE

As I may have mentioned elsewhere, two of my earliest memories are of the circus and professional wrestling. I can remember sitting in my grandparent's house, before my family even had a television, watching professional wrestling with my grandfather. He loved it and hence so did I. Growing up in New York, the wrestling we saw back then was the WWF, with stars such as Bruno Sammartino, Bobo Brazil and Killer Kowalski. Wrestling then was very different than today. Back then matches could last an hour or more and there was both skill and showmanship. Today, of course, matches rarely last more than ten minutes.

I followed wrestling throughout my young life and when I got to college, a group of us began following Gordon Solie and his Championship Wrestling from Florida promotion. Gordon served as the announcer and had stars such as Dusty Rhodes, Ric Flair, Killer Karl Kox and Barry Windham. Every Saturday morning all the guys got together to watch wrestling. We took it very seriously, memorizing the wrestler's favorite lines, and practicing their moves on each other while the TV played on. Gordon would close each show with us joining in, "So long from the Sunshine State!"

Little did any of us know back in September of 1975 that within a few months we would be working the shows with all the guys we watched on television.

One of my favorite stories of all time connects wrestling, my college life and a favorite alcoholic drink of the day called a Kamikaze. On a Friday night our school, Biscayne College, hosted a free cookout for all the students, which included not only food, but also all the "blue runners" we cared to drink. ("Blue runners" were our college code name for Busch beer, since it came in a blue can and after a few you had to run to the bathroom.) We decided to up the fun a bit by mixing pitchers of Kamikaze shooters and taking them along to the cookout. With nothing on our calendar for Saturday, except watching wrestling on TV at noon as usual, a large group of us got very intoxicated. Later that evening, some damage was done in the restrooms at the school. Since we had brought the liquor, we were, unknown to us, considered the suspects. (In reality, it wasn't us. With all we were drinking, we needed those restrooms!)

So, Saturday morning just after wrestling had started the phone rang. It was Father John Farrell, the president of the college. My dear friend, Rick Berry picked up the phone and answered, "Hello."

"Hello, this Father Farrell, president of Biscayne College, who is this please?"

"Rick Berry."

"Rick, I need to speak with you and your housemates over some damage done at the cookout last night."

"Father, I'd love to talk to you, but wrestling is on, so you'll have to call back after 1 o'clock." Click.

Rick had actually hung up on the president! Needless to say, we took our wrestling seriously.

I, of course, was excited to find myself working with professional wrestlers after 20 years of being a fan. The first show I remember working was at the Hollywood Sportatorium as the backstage manager there and two things still stand out in my mind. First was a world championship title match between the champion Harley Race and the incredible Andre the Giant, who I would get to work with a number of times including one of his last matches before his untimely death. Andre was truly the 8th Wonder of the World as he was billed. He was a giant and his escapades inside and outside the ring are legendary. His appetite was incredible as was his drinking ability. There are many stories of Andre drinking cases and cases of beer in a sitting and, at least once, passing out and having to be left in the bar until he awoke the next morning since no one could move an almost 8 foot tall, 600-pound sleeping giant. The night he wrestled a much smaller champion Harley Race I wondered how it could even be made to look competitive. As it turned out, it was one of the hardest fought, most brutal matches I have ever seen live or taped. Harley incredibly won the match. Both men won my respect for the pounding they took that evening.

But even more memorable was something that happened after the matches that night. Eddie Graham and his son Mike were both famous wrestlers; Eddie then in his mid-50s and his son Mike in his mid-20s. Eddie Graham was also the promoter of the event. On this evening he was not wrestling but his son Mike was. Sitting in the second row of the audience were two very large, very drunk redneck fellows, garbed in their blue jean overalls, swiggin' beer and spittin' tobacco. From the first moments on, for the two hours the show lasted, they called Eddie Graham every name in the book and when Mike Graham came out, the verbal harassment continued against both father and son. Eddie Graham came over to me and asked me to tell them if they wanted a piece of the Grahams to just stay after the matches. Eddie then told me to allow them to stay but make sure all the other customers were out of the building. With the show over and the crowd gone, these two lumbering oafs climbed into the ring.

Before they or I could react Mike Graham was in the ring and began pummeling the two guys. I don't think either one even got a punch in, and I don't think Eddie Graham even made it into the ring because by the time he got there both men were laying unconscious. It taught them the lesson that they should have known, it isn't a good idea to pick a fight with a professional fighter. I've always said that if there were to be a fight, I'd want a pro wrestler on my side, because although they pull their punches in the ring, they also know how to throw them in real life as well. A few of the staff carried them outside the front gates and deposited them on the sidewalk.

The days of "fake" blood and blood capsules in pro wrestling are, for the most part, gone. Most blood you see today is the result of the wrestlers cutting themselves with a hidden piece of razor blade, of scar tissue from previous cuts opening up, or actual bleeding from cuts inflicted by chair shots and the like. One of the bloodiest matches I ever worked occurred at the Miami Bayfront Center, a very unique facility that had the stands and seats on the bay bank, and the stage and in this case the ring floating out in the bay 10 yards or so from shore.

Professional wrestling loves to imitate the political climate. At the time Russia and Poland were violently fighting each other so of course wrestling followed suit with a match between "Polish Power" Ivan Putski and "The Russian Bear" Nikita Koloff. But this was not to be just a regular match, but a steel chain match with both wrestlers tethered together by a 20-foot steel chain around one wrist. Now Nikita Koloff wasn't even really Russian but these two guys went at it as if both were really standing up for their "own" country versus the hated rival. It truly was a war with each wrestler picking up the heavy chain and whipping the other over and over. The pain had to be excruciating and the entire ring was covered in blood. I don't remember who the eventual winner was, but both men had to be carried from the ring to the dressing rooms. I can't imagine how they must have felt the next day nor how they could have wrestled again within even the next week, if not longer.

For many matches I was the security guy walking the wrestlers to the ring. When you had the "good guys" it wasn't so bad, but when you were walking the "heels" out, you really had to be on your toes. People spit, threw beers and anything else they could find at the hated villains. The Ultimate Warrior was a big wrestling star who used to remind me I didn't need to get him to the ring, because once he was announced he ran to the ring at full speed and was afraid of tripping or bumping into his security ruining his entrance so he always went out alone.

One of my favorite memories was sitting backstage while two tag teams that "hated" each other warmed up, with all four of them on the floor doing pushups. They were the French Canadian Rougeau Brothers (Ray & Jacques) and The Rockers (Shawn Michaels and Marty Jannetty). Picture all four of these big men on the floor, shoulder to shoulder, doing push-ups while, of course, their storyline was that they hated each other. They had me laughing so hard with their banter back and forth I was almost crying. They were like little school girls. For maybe fifteen minutes it went on, back and forth. "Your haircuts look gay." "You never would even be here if you weren't kissing Vince's ass." (Vince being Vince McMahon, the owner of the WWE.) "Who makes your outfits, a clown?" "You really need to work out more; you are a lazy ass." Back and forth they went and I was just cracking up. Then it was time to go to the ring. The favored Rockers went out to great fanfare and with no problems. The hated French Rougeaus warned me that they had just purchased these new robes and didn't want any of the fans pulling on them or pulling the rhinestones off so to please watch them very carefully. And indeed people did try to grab at the villains, but we got them out to the ring without incident. I was standing ringside as the match progressed and predictably the bad guys won by cheating sending the crowd into an uproar.

I was escorting the Rougeaus back to the dressing room amidst the boos and thrown beers when I saw someone flying over my shoulder. I turned about to clothesline the guy thinking it was an irate fan, but at the last moment saw it was Rocker Shawn Michaels. I stopped my swing at the last instant as he flew over me on top the Rougeaus and started a brawl in the walkway to the delight of the fans. All I was trying to do was get out of the pile of bodies that included me, both Rougeaus and Shawn Michaels, while avoiding the fists flying in every direction. They got up and fought all the way back through the curtain leading backstage to the dressing room.

As soon as they were behind the curtain the fight stopped and they slapped each other on the back and headed for the showers. I stopped Shawn Michaels and we both started laughing. I told him I was ready to throw a punch and he said it would have killed him since he was in midair at the time. I told him I thought it was a crazy fan and was going to stop them at all costs. We laughed and high fived each other and I told him if he was ever going to jump over me again to at least let me know prior to the attack. Years later when Shawn Michaels screwed Bret Hart by not following the script on Bret's last day in the WWE before joining WCW, I thought back to the encounter and wished I had decked Shawn.

When the Orlando Arena first opened one of its first events was pro wrestling and on the card was my old friend Andre the Giant. He was at the end of his career and only had a few months to live but of course we didn't know that at the time. True pituitary giants like Andre always suffer from health problems, including circulatory problems and lack of stamina. At this point Andre was no different. By the time we walked from the dressing room to the ring, he already was gasping for air, exhausted. Climbing into the ring seemed a challenge. I truly felt sorry for him. But he was always the showman and you could tell he loved being in the ring in front of the fans. After the match I walked him back to the dressing room. While in public view we walked next to each other, but as soon as we got behind the curtain, he put his massive hand on my shoulder to steady himself to get back to the locker room. He said thanks and disappeared behind the door. That would be the last time I would see Andre the Giant. Someone recently gave me a DVD about Andre and it brought back lots of great memories.

Wrestling fans are a unique bunch. They love to cheer and they love to boo. I was working a show at the Sundome in Tampa and showed up wearing sweatpants and hooded sweatshirt top. Now the performers and backstage entrance is located down a tunnel to the lower level of the building. So wrestling fans would stand up above the tunnel behind a chain link fence to see their favorite wrestlers arrive. I parked up at the top of the ramp to the tunnel and walked down. As soon as I got out of my truck, people started booing me, calling me every name in the book, assuming I was a wrestler. I just put the hood up on my sweatshirt and continued in which only made the booing louder. "I hope you get killed you pig!" I remember hearing. I realized they thought I was a wrestler and decided I must be a bad guy. I was laughing all the way into the arena.

The first person I ran into inside was female wrestler and original WWE Diva Sensational Sherrie Martell, a WWE Hall of Famer. I had worked with her before and said, "Sherrie, come look at this! People are booing me!" She stayed just out of sight in the tunnel as I walked out in sight of the crowd and once they spotted me, the crowd started in again. Sherrie thought that was the funniest thing. She said, "Frank, you've already gotten over on them, you better get in the ring." At that point I was too old to begin a career as a villain in pro wrestling, but it was funny.

Later I brought out my dear friend and Sundome Manager John Mazzola and showed him the reaction. Now the crowd decided we were both wrestlers (both being big enough to be) and let us both have it. We laugh about that to this day. Sadly, my friend Sherrie Martell died early, like so many other pro wrestlers, at only 49 on June 15, 2007.

My next assignment that night was to supervise the "meet and greet" between Randy "Macho Man" Savage and some lucky fans. The first group I escorted backstage was a group of five car salesman who had won the chance to meet the Macho Man through a sales promotion where they worked. Typically, the wrestler would shake hands, pose for a few pictures, and sign a few autographs. I took them into the hallway and called Randy out from his dressing room. The salesman asked me to take a group picture of them with Randy. Two guys stood on each side of Randy and as I was about to snap the picture, the fifth guy jumped on Randy's back! Randy though he was being attacked and slammed the guy into the cement wall behind them. The other guys were stunned, as was I, as the salesman crumpled to the ground and Randy retreated to his dressing room, slamming the door behind him. To add insult to injury, the fallen salesman lay crumpled on the floor and a large picture from the wall fell on his head, breaking the glass, popping the picture out; so he lay there semiconscious and "framed" with his head sticking out through the glassless frame.

Owner of the New York Yankees George Steinbrenner is, among other things, a huge professional wrestling fan. I was working a television taping at the Sundome in Tampa, where normally I would be escorting wrestlers back and forth to the ring and monitoring other backstage operations. On this night I was asked to go meet Mr. Steinbrenner in the parking lot, escort him backstage, and then to his ringside seat for the matches.

As his limo pulled up, Mr. Steinbrenner exited the vehicle. I introduced myself to him and we walked in to the backstage area. Once we were backstage, of course, many of the wrestlers came up to him and either said hello or introduced themselves. What impressed me about Mr. Steinbrenner was each time a wrestler approached him, he introduced me as well. Some of the wrestlers knew me, but those that didn't had to think I was some VIP friend of George's.

As he and I were walking down the hallway, Hulk Hogan stepped out of his dressing room. He and George greeted each other as old friends and as before George introduced me to Hulk. Hulk said, "Wait a second, George, I want to introduce you to my dad," and Hulk called his dad out into the hallway. Introductions were made again with George again introducing me.

The cool thing about this was, every time I saw Hulk that night, he would say hi or slap me on the back as if I were someone important. In my later meeting with Hulk working both wrestling shows and a few of his other personal appearances, I would always remind him of the meeting with his dad and George. He always remembered it and treated me as an old friend rather than just an event worker.

Television tapings no longer happen the way they did on this occasion. Today shows are live and the taped shows are done one at a time in different arenas on different nights most of the time, selling lots of tickets at each event. Back in the "old days," three or four television shows would be taped in one night. Sometimes the show would start at, say, 7 p.m. and could last until the wee hours of the morning. All of the WWE (then the WWF) wrestlers would be there and many would wrestle three or four matches. With all the wrestlers backstage, it made for cramped quarters and none of the guys looked forward to their 10 minutes onstage, then hours off, then going on again, etc.

I was walking down one of the narrow hallways and a wrestler known as Virgil the Bodyguard was walking about ten feet ahead of me. Dressing rooms lined both sides of the narrow hallway and all of a sudden a hand came out of one of them and slapped Virgil on the back really hard. The hand quickly retreated back into the dressing room as Virgil spun around to see who hit him. All Virgil saw was me looking at him in an empty hallway and just as he was about to attack me, before I could say anything, wrestler Brutus "The Barber" Beefcake came out of the dressing room and Virgil quickly realized it was he, not I, who had hit him and they began chatting.

After their conversation I approached Virgil and after relating the story, he laughed and said "Yeah, I turned around and saw someone I didn't know who I thought had just hit me. I was gonna kill you." So I guess you could say that Brutus "The Barber" Beefcake saved my life.

Pro wrestling even affected me in other jobs that I held. While working as the resident magician at FAO Schwartz in Orlando, the other store employees marveled at the fact that most of the celebrities who visited the store knew me. Be it Shaquille O'Neal or Jeff Gordon, I could almost always go up and remind them where we met and go from there. But my favorites were, of course, the wrestlers who stopped by. Hulk Hogan, in full NWO makeup, came in, as did Scott Hall (usually in full Razor Ramon garb), Mike Rotundo, Earthquake and many others.

One of the worst jobs I ever had was as a multiplex movie theater manager. I hated every day of that job, except the day the security guard for the mall we were attached to, called me on the phone and told me to lock up my cash in the safe because "a Mexican gang" was in the mall. He told me they were headed towards the theater and they "seemed to be looking for trouble." Now I had never received a call like that before and started to think of what I should do as I got another call from the security guard saying they were on their way towards our box office.

Not sure of what to do next, I nervously stepped outside to get a glimpse of what was headed my way. I was in shock as I saw the "Mexican gang." Indeed they were all Hispanic and very tough looking. I shouted out, "Konan, what's up, bro?!" It was Konan, the professional wrestler, along with about a dozen other of the most famous

"Lucha Libre" wrestlers of the time. Wrestlers like El Parka, Eddie and Chavo Guerrero, Ray Mysterio, Psycosis, Super Crazy and others. They were all wrestling for the WCW at that time and filming their TV shows at Disney. Needless to say I told them they were my guests anytime at the theater and they would on occasion bring me tickets to matches.

In its heyday the WCW promotion taped their TV shows at Disney-MGM Studios in Orlando and if you reserved free seats by calling ahead, you got in to see the show and the park afterwards for free. My daughter Shannon, who was four or five at the time, and I would go quite often. Knowing many of the guys, we always got great seats and the guys treated Shannon like a little VIP. Brett Hart would always take his sunglasses off and put them on her, Hulk Hogan gave her his shirt, and Hacksaw Jim Duggan gave her one of his trademark 2x4s. At one of these tapings, we were seated in the front row watching the WCW trainer Dwayne Bruce, a.k.a. Sgt. Buddy Lee Parker, taking a beating in the ring from Big Sexy Kevin Nash. Now Buddy, er, Dwayne was short, but built like a fireplug and his character was that of a policeman. During the match I was heckling him quite a bit. When the match ended as he walked by me I said, "You know what you'd be if you were six inches taller and fifty pounds heavier?" I was kind of surprised when he said, "No, what?" and I replied, "Still a loser!" The fans around me were laughing and he got nose-to-nose with me. The first thing he did was wink at me and I could tell by the look in his eyes, this was all for show. But we started yelling at each other, him threatening to hit me while the crowd went nuts.

The funniest part of the story is when we arrived home the first thing my daughter did was run to my wife and say, "Mommy, Daddy got in a big fight with a policeman today!" Before my wife got too upset, I explained this whole story to her.

I couldn't leave a chapter on wrestling without mentioning my favorites so I have to start with "The Nature Boy" Ric Flair, Dusty Rhodes "The American Dream", Andre the Giant, King Kong Bundy and my friend Barry Windham, a great wrestler in his own right and son of Wrestling Hall of Famer Black Jack Mulligan. And of all the memorabilia that I own from all the entertainment industry, I think my most prized possession is the program from the wrestling event, "The Last Tangle in Tampa" (August 3, 1980). On the cover is a picture of the two combatants in the main event, Dusty Rhodes and Harley Race who would wrestle for the World championship. Both of these Hall of Fame legends have signed it to me and I treasure it.

Author & Randy Savage

The Nature Boy Ric Flair & Author

Jeff Jarrett, Author, Miss Deborah, and the late
Owen Hart

Kurt Angle & Author

Pro Wrestling's Legendary
MICK FOLEY

Author & Mick Foley

CHAPTER 29
GOLDEN OLDIES

Over the years I worked quite a few "oldies" shows and reunions with a number of the groups and singers from the 1950s and 1960s. I remember so many great performances from people like Lou Christie ("Lightning Strikes"), Dion ("Runaround Sue"), Frankie Valli ("Let's Hang On") and so many more. Three of my all time favorites that I have worked for and seen as a fan are Bo Diddley, The Coasters and Peter, Paul & Mary.

Bo Diddley is an American original. A valid argument could be made there would be no rock and roll without the familiar guitar riffs invented by Bo. There is no rock guitarist that doesn't recognize him as the Godfather of Rock. Sitting and talking to Bo Diddley was one of the greatest pleasures I have ever had. He was an incredible person, legendary performer and story teller par excellence. Although he could discuss music at any level, he was just as entertaining telling you about a recent horror movie he saw (his favorite movie genre) or about his love of cooking, especially his fried chicken. Bo had to learn to cook because back in the days of segregation, many times he found himself playing clubs that would not allow him to eat or even be in the club except for his performance. He would tell of turning down millions of dollars to open a chain of fried chicken restaurants that he claims would have been called "Bo Diddley's Ass Kickin' Chicken." I think it would have been a huge success.

Another story Bo told me was that he had invented a car that ran without gasoline. Now exactly how or what it ran on, I'm not sure. He never disclosed that, but as he told you the story, you really started to believe him! I still remember the end of the story that had Bo burying the miracle car on his ranch because he said too many government and oil executive types were snooping around asking questions. With today's gas prices, I wish we had that car!

Having worked a few of his shows, I saw he was coming to Orlando to play The Peabody Hotel's Sunset Concert Series. These were great shows put on by The Peabody that showcased all kinds of entertainers on their huge outdoor pool deck. I arrived early with my then new 8mm video camera and there was Bo onstage warming up on the drums, talking to his band, etc. I began filming and a few minutes later he called me over. He asked me, "Did I give you permission to film me?"

"No, sir," I answered.

"Is that one of those new 8mm cameras?"

"Yes, sir."

"It has sound on it, right?"

"Yes, sir."

"You going to send me a copy of it?"

"Yes, sir," and suddenly I had all access for the show and taped what I could with one battery, always worrying it would run out. I managed to get Bo on drums, a bit of him chatting and parts of the show that night. He gave me his address and telephone number and not only did send him the tape, but also called and talked to him occasionally.

Because of his popularity, the Peabody had Bo back the next year. Of course, I went. Arriving early, I went up and chatted with Bo for awhile before the show. The emcee went onstage and started Bo's introduction and Bo took the stage to thunderous applause. He approached the microphone for the first time and said, "Where's my friend, Frank Lynch?" Not knowing what was going on, I raised my hand and waved and he said, "Come up on stage, boy." Embarrassed, I walked onstage and Bo turned away from the mike and handed me a tiny tape recorder. "I bought this in Japan yesterday. It's supposed to tape continuously without you having to turn the tape over. Tape the show for me and give it back to me afterward." He handed me the little recorder, leaned back into the mike, and said, "My friend, Frank Lynch everybody," and the audience clapped. Then he started his incredible show.

Bo passed away in June of 2008, but I consider meeting him and being called his friend a great honor, because without Bo and his legendary square guitar, there would not be rock music as we know it today. Make it a point to listen to at least one Bo Diddley song, listen to that familiar guitar chord progression and realize that he was the man that invented it. Bo Diddley is and always will be one of the greatest.

A group that truly deserves their place in the Rock and Roll Hall of Fame is The Coasters who were inducted in 1987. You may remember songs like "Charlie Brown," "Poison Ivy" and so many more hits. Although many think of them as a classic doo-wop group, they are quick to correct this and explain they are a rock and roll group, not a doo-wop group. I have worked many Coasters shows over the years as well as being a big fan. There are many imposter groups out there, but the real Coasters are the group that is led by Carl Gardner Sr. and Carl Gardner Jr. based out of South Florida. Anytime I see a venue advertising The Coasters, I always call them to see if it is the real Coasters, and if they are not, I let the sponsoring venue know that. My little contribution to the purity and history of rock and roll, I guess.

Every member of The Coasters is a true gentleman and appreciates every person in the audience. I have never seen them give a bad performance. On my fortieth birthday, I was lucky enough to spend the evening going to a Coasters concert at a now defunct venue called Little Darlin's in Kissimmee, Florida. The Coasters were gracious enough to recognize me from the stage and wish me a happy birthday. An even bigger thrill was going to see them on my forty-fifth birthday with my whole family. Again The Coasters were so gracious and pleased, maybe even shocked to see my daughters, Shannon then 11 and Diana then 8, sitting there singing along to every song, amidst a crowd of adults. With it becoming a tradition, I was also lucky enough to see the Coasters for my fiftieth birthday in Clermont, Florida. Sadly, Carl Gardner Sr. is now semi-retired but his son Carl Jr. carries on the tradition proudly with the other members of the legendary Coasters.

I wanted to thank, in this printed, timeless forum, this group of entertainers who have given so much to the world of music and also to myself and my family. So thank you, Carl Gardner Sr., Carl Gardner Jr., Al Morse, J.W Lance, "Mr. Bass Man" Ronnie Bright and legendary guitarist "Curly" Palmer. If you ever get a chance to see them, by all means do, you are not only watching an incredibly talented singing group but music history.

The last group I need to mention here is the legendary trio of Peter, Paul & Mary. When I was a young boy the first songs I learned to play on a guitar were Peter, Paul & Mary songs. Their effect on folk music, and in helping to change things for the better in the turbulent 60s, can not be overlooked. For instance, the group played live at Martin Luther King's "If I Had A Dream" speech rally! Perhaps as amazingly, a Peter, Paul & Mary concert today is as inspiring as ever. Songs like "If I Had a Hammer" and "Puff the Magic Dragon" will simply live on forever. And these three performers are among the warmest, most down to earth people you could ever meet.

My best memory of the many concerts I witnessed was one that I attended as a guest with my wife Barb and daughter Shannon who then was about four years old. Mary was telling the audience, "You know, it's amazing, but on occasion when we begin to play this next song, as soon as the first note is sounded, a child will yell out the name of the song. They can name this song in one note!" When the first note was plucked on the big bass viola on stage, Shannon, sitting in the third row, yelled out "It's Puff! It's Puff!" Mary started laughing and said, "See!" and the audience laughed as indeed the first note that had been played was from "Puff the Magic Dragon."

Proudly hanging on my wall is an autographed picture from Peter, Paul & Mary and it is inscribed "To Frank, in peace, in thanks, in love" and signed by the three troubadours. In reality we should thank them for their contributions to peace, thank them for decades of meaningful music, and show them the love they deserve for who they are and what they have done for music and the world as a whole. Again, if ever given the chance, go to a Peter, Paul & Mary concert, there is no way you could not enjoy it.

Bo Diddley

Carl Gardner of The Coasters & Author

CHAPTER 30
GAMBLING FOR FUN & PROFIT

From my college days on, I found fun and profit in the casinos, dog tracks, jai alai frontons and horse tracks that I came upon. While at college in Miami, we would attend the dog tracks for a fun night out. Early on it somehow became a tradition that when the carload of us stopped to pay the one dollar parking fee to the parking attendant, we would all bark like the dogs we would soon be betting on. Although it must have shocked the attendant, we somehow convinced ourselves it was our good luck charm to a winning night. Gamblers are a strange lot.

I am much more serious and wealthier from studying and playing casino blackjack, 21. I have seriously studied a couple of methods and can card count. As long as I am not recognized by the dealer or pit boss as a card counter, I usually do really well at the game. If I am recognized as a card counter, I am asked to leave the casino. When I go to a table, I am there to win and take things very seriously. Nothing bothers me more than the recreational gambler who comes up to the table and says "Well, I have another $500 to lose." If they are there to lose money, they can just give it to me. I am not a fun person at a blackjack table.

I can remember winning a blackjack tournament, and because of the circumstances and my "win at all cost" table personality, being very happy my sizeable brother was at my back. When I entered the tournament I knew many of the dealers, which is of no significance except other players took exception to the friendliness between us. I was one of the first players in and one of the first eliminated. All the other players were happy to see me go. But then one of the pit bosses said they had a cancellation and if I wanted to re-enter the tournament I could by paying another $1000 entry fee.

I wasn't going to re-enter but the pit boss said to me, "Frank, you know you are a better player than you just showed." So, of course, I coughed up another grand. This time my luck was much better and as player after player dropped out, I found myself at the final table with just a few hands left and I realized I good shot at winning the tournament. Luckily about this time my younger brother Tim wandered by and I said out loud, "Tim, hang around. I am about to win this tournament." Of course this didn't sit well with the other players.

One of the rules written in tiny letters on the tournament rules board was that a player can ask for a chip count at any time. So, jerk that I am some might say, as we got closer to the last hands, I asked for a chip count from every player on every hand. There were some very, very angry card players at that table. I did this for two reasons, first it was playing with my opponents emotions and, more importantly, I knew what I had to bet and when to win the tournament.

With all my calculations behind me, I knew going into the last hand, I was the odds on favorite to win the tournament mathematically. So, true to my table persona, I announced before the last hand, "I win, I win! Sorry, folks, but it's all over! I am the champion!" There were players at the table saying "Not so fast!" and "Not yet, I'm going to take you out, a--hole!" However, I knew, barring a miracle, I would win with the proper bet regardless what the others at the table did. So I continued my celebration through the last hand, luckily with my large, looming brother at my back, and did indeed win the tournament.

I was the only happy player in the casino, as others complained I was friends with the dealers, had entered twice and somehow knew I was going to win before it was all over. I loved it. Sore losers! And, of course, having my brother celebrating at my side probably helped me get out of there safely with my cash too! Thanks Tim-o!

One of the many jobs I've had over the years that I really enjoyed was as a pari-mutuel teller at Gulfstream Racetrack in Hollywood, Florida. The tellers are the men (or women) that you place your bets with at a racetrack. In order to become a teller you needed to attend classes, pass a test and then be accredited by the State of Florida. I attended the classes and was scheduled for my test at 7 a.m. on a Saturday morning.

I arrived early and was feeling a bit nervous, so I walked down to the racetrack and began watching the horses in their morning workouts with the tiny jockeys on their backs. I was standing at the rail, watching a horse in full gallop approach and just as he reached me, I heard what sounded like a gunshot. The horse stumbled a bit and then stood there, maybe ten feet away from me. I looked at him and saw that one of his rear legs had come completely off his body and was laying there next to him. The "gunshot" I had heard was the horse breaking his leg and the gruesome consequences. This really shook me up, but an old-timer standing by me said, "Don't worry about that, kid. That horse was so doped up he never knew it happened." He may have been right because as they brought out the wagon to remove the poor horse from the track, he stood there as if nothing was wrong. Either he was doped up or in severe shock or maybe both. Either way, it's an image that stays with me to this day. The horse was put down and I went in, very shook up, and somehow passed my test to become a licensed pari-mutuel teller in Florida.

Pari-mutuel tellers in Florida were unionized. In order to break into the union, you had to work 10 days during a racing season. I quickly learned they didn't let anyone work more than nine days a season, so they didn't have to admit you to the union. All the union workers worked every day, but we had to show up and wait to see if they called our name. In my case, if they did then great, I worked, and if not I would have a fun day at the track. I worked three seasons at Gulfstream, working nine days a season and loved every minute of it. Looking back it may have been a good thing I never worked the required ten days, because had I broken into the union, I probably would have spent my whole life taking and making bets at the horse tracks, jai alai frontons and dog racing tracks in Florida.

As I said I had great fun working, taking bets and making them. Of course you had to be very careful when making bets. It was legal for us to place bets at our own machines and most tellers did it. The problem came if you made bets and didn't have the money to cover them if you didn't win. A guy working next to me on the first race of the day, with no money in his wallet, placed a $10 bet on the favorite horse to win. The horse came in second so he now owed his cash drawer $10. On the second race he bet $50 on the favorite horse to place (come in first or second to win the bet.) The horse didn't place so he was now down $60. Race three he bets on the favorite horse to show (come in first, second or third to get paid) with a hundred dollar bet! You guessed it, the horse didn't show and the teller was short $160 in his cash drawer. At this point, a track official and the track security guards appeared. They counted his drawer and asked for the $160 he owed. When he said he had no money, he was handcuffed and taken away, arrested on a felony charge of pari-mutuel theft. Needless to say I was very careful with my own bets when I worked after that.

Aside from being able to bet on the races, the job was very lucrative even if you weren't picking winners. You were paid $100 per racing day, a few hours work, which was a lot back in the mid-seventies and most horse players gave you tips. When a player won say $5.20 or $9.60, most would leave the change as a tip. Although it doesn't sound like much, when multiplied by the hundreds of bets paid off in a day it really added up. When someone won big, say $235 on a two dollar bet, most players would leave a $5 or $10 tip.

I remember my favorite bettor well. She was a seventy-year-old woman that fit the description of "bag lady" perfectly. I enjoyed talking to my bettors and many would come back to me race after race or ask where I had been when I didn't work for awhile. On this lucky day, my bag lady came up and bet $5 on the first race. I teased her saying, "I'm only selling winners today, ma'am." Her bet won that first race and she was paid back $11.50. She left me the 50 cents as a tip and bet the next race, which she won again and again left the change. Her winning streak continued as she would bet with me and collect from me leaving me a good tip, race after race. I was beginning to follow her bets, bet the same bets myself and was all in all having a great day, as was she.

In the tenth race, my bag lady bet a five dollar trifecta. At this point I was way ahead on the day and didn't bet the long shot trifecta. I should have, because the bet won and paid $6753.20! I thought all was not lost because after all the tips she had left me all day, both on the horses and in cash, how much would she leave me on this huge win?! She came up saying, "Frank, you really are my good luck charm!" and handed me the winning ticket. I slowly counted out the $6753.20 wondering if she would leave me the $53 or more. Inexplicably, she took every penny, said, "Thank you. See you next time!" and was gone! Gamblers are a funny lot.

CHAPTER 31
DRAG STRIPPERS

This is not a chapter about transsexual nude dancers, but about the drivers who make up the professional drag racing circuit. While backstage manager of the Hollywood Sportatorium, I also helped operate the Hollywood International Speedway located next door to the arena. Prior to working here I had never been to a live drag race event but I did know of the famous drivers of the time from seeing them on television. Drivers I then interacted with, like Shirley "Cha Cha" Muldowney, Don "The Snake" Prudhomme and "Big Daddy" Don Garlits.

My job was a simple one. I sat at the end of the drag strip in a little shack with a two-way radio and little slips of paper. At the end of each race, a voice on the radio would tell me the drivers name and his (or her) "ET," elapsed time, the time it took them to run the quarter-mile track. Seems simple, right? I get to watch the races from the ET shack and hand out the times to the drivers. What would really happen always amazed me. Unless it was a world record or close to it, EVERY driver assumed I made a mistake on their time. They would start screaming at me and I would usually say, "Don't shoot the messenger," as I was only relaying what I had been told. This would only make them madder. I was called every name in the book, had scores of racing helmets thrown at me and more than once was told I was going to be run over the next time they raced. Luckily that never happened and I enjoyed my days in the ET shack at the races.

One of the staples at the track was Benny "Boom Boom" Koske. He was a great attraction and had nothing to do with racing. I loved his act. He would come out in a red, white and blue jumpsuit and climb into a coffin with a helmet on. Safety first. His assistants would then load sticks of dynamite into the coffin. After a "safety check," the countdown would begin and at zero the dynamite would explode splintering the coffin and leaving Benny a seemingly lifeless body on the now bare ground with smoke all around him. As his aides rushed to his side, he would stagger to his feet and stumble off to the thunderous cheers of the crowds. It was a great act and I've always wondered if I could recreate it.

CHAPTER 32
SON OF SAM

This book and all the experiences in it might never have happened if the notorious killer Son of Sam, David Berkowitz, had his way. Only by chance did I survive his possible onslaught.

Arriving in my native New York from Florida for a few weeks vacation in the summer of 1977, Son of Sam was on the minds of many people in New York City, but there certainly was little or no fear in the Hamptons where I was.

I had invited friends of mine out for the weekend to hit the beach during the day and the clubs at night. One of the most famous, or infamous, clubs was The Mad Hatter in East Quogue, just a few miles from my home. The long weekend happy hours featured 50 cent mixed drinks, five beers for a dollar, and free hot dogs, as well as live bands. The club itself had a large interior with five bars and a stage and a large outdoor patio area. "Our" table was always outside on the patio close to one of the outside bars and the free hot dogs.

As was our practice, we left my house at about 12:45 in the afternoon on Sunday, August 7, so we would be walking in just as the club opened, and wouldn't have to fight the crowds that would arrive later in the afternoon. On this particular day, as I drove down Montauk Highway with my friends in the car, we noticed we were racing a large dark cloud that had all the makings of a big thunderstorm. As we pulled up to the Mad Hatter, we hurried to the entrance to beat the raindrops.

As soon as we got inside, it started to pour. The skies seemingly just opened up and there was torrential rain for about an hour or more. Normally by this time there would have been hundreds of people at the bar, but this Sunday there were only a handful, happily partying inside while the storm raged on outside. Many, many drinks were consumed and a good time was had by all despite the weather.

On August 10, 1977, a mere three days later, David Berkowitz, Son of Sam was captured. As police questioned him about his movements and plans and read his diary, they found out that on that past Sunday, Son of Sam had driven out to East Quogue with a machine gun in his trunk. He told the police his plan was to drive out to the Mad Hatter, pull into the parking lot, take out the machine gun and mow down all the people partying on the patio. He had indeed driven out to the Hatter, but when he got there and it was raining with no one on the patio, had turned around and drove the two hours back to New York City.

Had the sun been out, there would have been more than a hundred people on the patio and most assuredly, my friends and I would have had our usual outside table right in the middle of it all. And had the sun been shining, also most assuredly, I would have been killed that day and most of my life experiences never would have happened. All I can say is it was a little bit of good karma.

CHAPTER 33
YOU GOTTA HAVE FRIENDS

I am a firm believer in "what goes around comes around." And throughout my life there have been many people whose good karma has helped me along and I will try and thank some of them here. If you aren't mentioned here, accept my apologies now for inadvertently omitting you. I'll get you in the next book.

First there are the surviving members of my family and extended family who for the most part have stuck with me through it all...

Thanks to my mom, Jean Lynch, who knew I walked to a different drummer and never tried to discourage it (too much). She never knew quite what to tell her friends when they asked what it was I do for a living. Now she can simply tell them I'm an author.

To my sister Erin and brother Tim, for all we went through that made us who we are.

And my Long Island nieces and nephews, hey, your crazy uncle wrote a book!

To my wife Barbara, how she has stuck by me through it all is beyond my belief, and to the two best kids a Dad could ever have, Shannon and Diana who I hope, from watching me, realize it's more important to be happy than anything else.

And to all my other blood relatives alive at the time of this writing, Father Francis Filmanski, Aunt Fran Filmanski, cousins, second cousins and the rest. I wish we were all closer but thanks for helping shape me during my youth in our extended family.

And to my second family in McSherrystown, Pennsylvania, the best in-laws a guy could want. "Mom" Cel Murphy, one of the original "Two Guys" Joe Murphy, Tom Murphy, Lisa Wolf and all my nieces and nephews, you are all great.

And to all my good friends who have remained that way either in reality or spirit, thanks for being a part of the three-ring circus that has been my life. Friends including Chris Kavan, Lewis and LuEllen Briguglio, Gary and Wendy Erwin, John Thorne, Billy Shunk, Bob Bender and to a whole group of friends who started with me in kindergarten and went through senior year as Westhampton Beach Hurricanes, folks like Kathy Lavelle, Donna Zaloom, Pat Abbott, Douglas Galanter, Linda Derryberry, Pam Follett, Laurie Culver, Judy Lomas and my "Air Force friends" like

Janet Loughlin, Stan Conte, Darryl Thomas, Jeff Sauter and Tom Collins.

And all of you who helped shape my life: Theodora Nowak Guzzi, Jeannie Gibson, Tom Pegues, Lou Padavan, Lew Walitz, Carrie Sevilla, Lisbeth Ann Dahlen, Andrew Martin, Kathy Wishbow O'Neill, and Valentina Cappazolli Hadland.

Then there all the Biscayne College Bobcats, Rick Berry, Justin Barrett, Kevin "Pie" Bell, John Mazzola, Mike Babcock, John Durnien, "Miami" Mike Deitche, Fr. Ed Sullivan, Fr. Joe "I teach by intimidation" Walsh, Joanne Carlino, "Uncle" Al Twitchel, Marylou Robinson, Freddie Mondi, and, of course, the late great staffs at Beefsteak Charlies, Art Stock's Playpen, and Crazy Greg's Button On The Beach.

And since friends like Rick Illobre, everyone from Ft. Lauderdale's former Pierce St. Annex, Jim Rousmanoff, Billy Q, Jack Blank, Rob Adams, Hillary Horner, Shawn Fernandez, Kelly Puckett, Mel Mogul, Linda Stone, Corby Day, Metal Mike Lever, Roscoe the Clown, Gini Valbuena, Rob Buback, Bridgette Porto, Paul Porto and the entire staff at Portoland, Greg Maher, Craig Young, and my editor Jessica Daniels, I couldn't have done it without you.

CHAPTER 34
THE FINAL CURTAIN

I want to thank everyone who reads this book. I hope the stories come across as well as they do when I tell them orally. There are still more stories to tell and more life situations to experience. I can only think to end this with the words of the Royal Hanneford Circus' owner, the lovely Struppi Hanneford, who always reminds us, "Never say goodbye, just say until next time," and may all your days be circus days!